DANGEROUS SECRETS

BROOKE SUMMERS

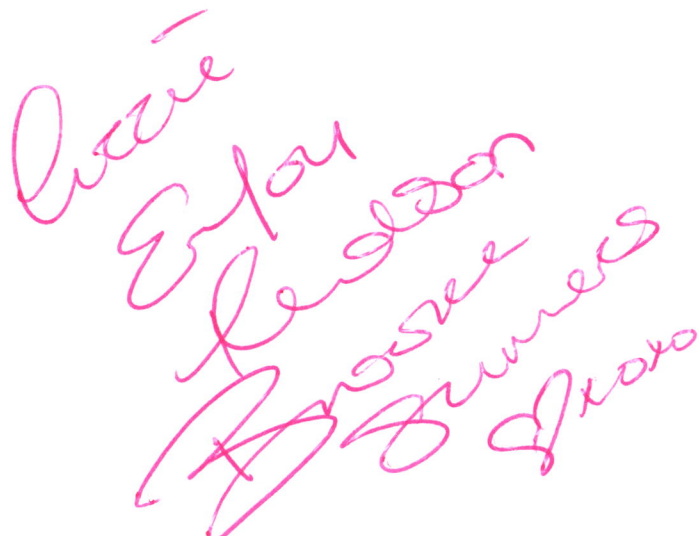

Dangerous Secrets

Part Two of the Kingpin Series

BROOKE SUMMERS

DANGEROUS SECRETS
First Edition published in 2020
Text Copyright © Brooke Summers

All rights reserved.

The moral right of the author has been asserted.

Cover Design by Lee Ching of Undercover Designs.
Formatter Kristine Moran of word bunnies.
Editing by Lisa Flynn of Simply Writing.
Proofread by Kristine Moran of word bunnies

No part of this publication may be reproduced, stored in or introduced into a retrieval system, or transmitted, in any form or by any means (electronic, mechanical, photocopying, recording or otherwise), nor be otherwise circulated in any form of binding or cover other than that in which it is published without the prior written permission of the author. Any person who does any unauthorized act in relation to this publication may be liable to criminal prosecution and civil claims for damages.
All characters in this publication are fictitious and any resemblance to real persons, living or dead, is purely coincidental.

ONE

Hudson
———————

PAIN, that's all I feel. An emptiness inside, as though I've lost everything. My pulse is pounding. Ringing in my ears is all that I can hear. I'm standing here in silence, looking at the blood on the floor, she's gone. That's all that's going through my mind. Someone has taken her, and I need her back. She's been gone for God knows how long now and I already feel as though I'm drowning. I've never felt this way before, like I have no control over what's going on.

"Jag," I call out through gritted teeth.

"Boss?" he replies, his voice deep and his eyes menacing. "What do you need?"

"Find me Juan," I demand. I know I have everyone on this but I need Jagger, right now he's the only man I trust to help me find her.

"I'm on it boss. I'm going to find her. Hudson, we will get her back." It's a promise

I nod, she left our parent's house because of the shit that she found out. She didn't call me; she ran, it's something I didn't think she would do. I thought she would at least talk to me first, let me explain everything but she didn't. Now she's gone.

"Boss you need to call Tina, she needs to know that Mia is gone. Get Barney and your Dad here. We need every available man on this." Jagger tells me, but quickly straightens himself after he realizes that he's gone too far.

I shake my head. "Dad and Barney are to stay where they are. Unless Barney wants to swap with someone so that he can be here to find Lacey? If someone's taken Mia, then there's a good chance they're going to go after the rest of my family. I can't let that happen, I won't let that happen. But right now, I have to make a phone call."

He nods agreeing with me. "I guess you're right. The last thing we need is for others to go missing. Although I don't think Barney needs to be there, your dad's more than one capable of taking care of himself. Are you going to call your mom? I'll make some calls. Juan can't be too hard to find. The man's a bastard."

"I'll visit her soon. It's funny, mom wasn't surprised when I told her about what Mia means to me and she's been looking forward to meeting her." She'll understand what it means that Mia's been taken. She'll also know what it's doing to me, and what kind of man this will turn me into, after all I am her son. I am my father's son. She never wanted me to be this but she accepted that it was who I was destined to be. I'll tell her about Mia and knowing mom she'll want to help find her. First things first I need to call Tina.

"Okay boss, call me if you need me." Jagger says as we walk out of the house, he walks to his car and climbs in.

I glance to the empty space where my car should have been, shit, I should have realized that Martin would have used it. Walking to Mia's car, I try the handle, a silent prayer on my lips. Thank God, it opens instantly. The keys are dangling from the ignition, the black and yellow ASU college keyring grinning inanely at me as it dangles, mocking me. Why don't you know where she is? It seemed to say. Weren't you supposed to protect her? She would have been safer if you weren't in her life. All the things that have been running through my mind continuously.

I shake my head at her leaving the keys in the ignition that shit has to stop. She can't be doing shit like that, especially in a neighborhood like this

As soon as I climb into the car, I'm surrounded by her, my jaw clenches as I smell her perfume, Lady Millions by Paco Rabanne. The seat being so far forward reminds me of her petite frame, my mind spins with different scenarios of what's happening to her as I adjust the position of the seat. The engine purrs and I put it into drive. Reaching into my pocket, I pull out my cell and place it in the cell holder. I dial my dad and hit call, putting it on speaker as it calls. "Son, did you find her?" He asks, not sounding too worried.

"Is Tina there?" I ask, my voice tight, it's her fault that Mia's gone. She was safe in Hidden Hills, but Tina had to open her mouth and she fled.

He is silent for a moment. "Yes, is everything okay?"

I pinch the bridge of my nose, not wanting to listen to him right now. "Put Tina on the phone." I growl through gritted teeth, my fingers clenched around my cell holding it tight.

"Hudson, what is it?" The disdain in her voice is still there but it's mixed with worry.

"I got to the house and she was gone. There's blood on the ground and the door was ajar. Someone has taken her." My breathing is ragged as I tell her.

"Gone?" She breathes.

"Yes." I say through gritted teeth, "She's gone."

A wail rings out and I bite my tongue, "Hudson, what's going on?" My dad asks and I roll my eyes at the over dramatic wailing coming from Tina.

"Mia was gone when I got to the house." I'm so fucking pissed right now, if Tina gave a shit about her daughter this wouldn't have happened. "Calm her down, I need to talk to her, having her screaming and wailing isn't going to help." I know that I sound harsh but I don't care, I need to find Mia.

Dad sighs, "Hudson her daughter is missing what do you think she's going to do?"

I scoff, "Dad, she didn't give a fuck when she was telling Mia everything about me. I told you before, Tina is selfish and she doesn't care about anyone but herself," I say through gritted teeth, why the hell am I having to say this shit? "Just get her to compose herself, I need some questions answered."

I hear whispering in the background, a couple of moments later he's back on the phone. "Okay son, you're on speaker, ask any questions you have."

I don't waste any time. "After you spoke to Mia, what happened?" There's a bite to my voice, one that I've used many times before and each and every time I get all the answers I need.

I can hear sniffing and I know that Tina is about to say something. "She didn't really say much. Then she ran out the house and I haven't heard from her since."

"You shouldn't have said anything to her. This is on you, she's gone because of *you*." My tone is quiet, I'm seething, Mia would have been fine had Tina not opened her damn mouth.

"Me? This is all on you. Mia would be here with me if you hadn't come along. Hudson you are the reason my daughter is gone. I just pray you find her, when you do I want you to keep the hell away from her."

I grind my teeth, biting back my response, this isn't the time to be arguing. "I'm going to find her and, make no mistake, when I do hell is going to be paid." My nostrils flare as I intake a sharp breath, trying to keep my composure.

"Dad?"

"Yes, Son?" he says instantly.

"Take me off speaker," I tell him, not wanting Tina to hear this part. This is business and she has nothing to do with it.

"Done." I can hear him walking, "What's going on?"

"Something isn't sitting right."

"Talk to me." Yeah he understands, he knows that there's more to this than meets the eye.

"When I first got into the house and realized that Mia and Lacey were gone I assumed that was Juan."

"And you don't now?" There's no judgment in his voice. That makes a change.

"I'm not sure. This is too sophisticated to be Juan's idea. I think there's more to play here and I can't figure out what." I've never been so honest with my dad before about my feelings. I'm the boss, I should have seen this coming, I should know who has her.

"Son, you're going to find her." I shake my head in disgust, he didn't say *we*, he said *you're*. He has no intention of helping me. I shouldn't be surprised, but yet I am. I didn't think my dad could stoop so low, and yet here we are.

"Yeah I will," I say with so much conviction I will not rest until I find her… find them.

"Call me if or when you have any news," he tells me sounding disinterested.

"Sure." I end the call. My temper is rising but I should've known that my dad will be no help. There is one person though who is always guaranteed to listen and offer a bit of insight.

Ten minutes later I'm pulling into my mom's drive. After switching off the engine I see she's sitting on the porch in her little rocking chair. Noticing me she looks up, a frown marring her face. When she recognizes it's me, her face lights up. She's wearing makeup, it's been a very long time since I saw my mom look so polished. Her hair is done for the first time in months, gone is the grey that grew from the roots, it's now replaced with black. Not only has her appearance changed but so has the color of the house. It used to be a dirty white color and unkempt whereas now, it's a bright white. I frown when I realize that the lawn has been mowed. Damn, have I entered the twilight zone?

"Hudson, what a pleasant surprise," she says with a bright smile as she gets up off the chair and walks over to me with her arms open wide waiting for me to walk into them. She's wearing a fitted dress and heels. They look out of place. When her and dad's marriage ended she started wearing sweats. I don't remember the last time I saw mom looking so well.

I smile at her as her arms enclose around me. "Hey, Mom."

She makes a tutting noise. "What's your father done now?"

I fight the urge to smile. "What hasn't he done?" Mom laughs. I take a seat on the chair beside her rocking chair. "Mom, Mia's been taken." It guts me to say it. I still can't believe she's gone. I can't believe I wasn't there to protect her. I should have been. She was supposed to be safe.

Mom gasps. "Hudson?" Tears swimming in her eyes. "How?"

I shrug. "I've no idea. Mom, I don't know who took her. I feel useless I don't know where to look. I have my suspicions, but even then I don't think they're right. My gut's screaming at me that there's more to it, but my brain can't think. It's like I'm in a fog. I can't see clearly, Mom."

"Hudson," she says slowly as she comes to take a seat beside me. "Deep breath. Take a deep breath, you need to take a step back and be the Boss."

I stare at her, this isn't what I thought this conversation was going to be like.

Mom laughs at me. "Hudson you're my boy. I know you better than you know yourself. Right now you're coming apart at the seams. Usually if something happens you know how to deal with it because it doesn't affect you, you know how to deal with everyone else. Hudson this is Mia we're talking about. She's your princess and that means she's yours." Her hand gently touches my cheek. "Right now you're acting like Mia's man. But baby boy, that's not going to help anyone." She grasps my hand, squeezing it as she looks at me, her eyes full of unshed tears. "Hudson, you're the Boss for a reason. It's time to remember that."

I understand what she means, it's just difficult thinking about anything else other than getting Mia back.

"Hudson I don't know how it all works, not anymore. When your father and I first got together, I knew how everything worked but since then it's changed and it's changed even more since you've taken over. But one thing remains the same, you are the Boss. You run this town, so start acting like it." Her smile is wide, she's trying to help which is a hell of a lot more than what dad's trying to do.

"My men are on this, Mom. I have everyone looking for her and looking for the man I believe could have a part in this. I am being the Boss, because that is who I am."

She shakes her head. "Yes, you are the boss. It is who you are. That's not who you are being now. You're distraught Hudson, anyone looking at you can see it. You're still that badass that you have the reputation of being, but to me, your mother, I can see that you're on the edge of breaking. I know what Mia means to you, which means I also know how this is affecting you. You're not in the right frame of mind to focus and that needs to change. If you want to find Mia, your mind-set needs to change."

I blow out a deep breath, she's right. I'm not in the right mind-set, but fuck if I'll let anyone know it.

"Talk to me, there's something you're not telling me. You said your gut's screaming at you. What is it telling you?" she's pleading with me, she wants to help and right now I think the best thing for me to do is take that help.

"Okay," I tell her and her face lights up. "I hadn't told Mia the truth about me. About what I do."

Her shoulders sag. "Oh Hudson, why?"

I'm not admitting to why. I didn't tell her because I wanted her to fall in love with me first, that way she would have stayed. That worked out fucking well didn't it? "Tina told her." I can't keep the contempt out of my voice when I say her name.

"Why? What did she gain out of telling her?"

"I don't know, all I do know is that woman is a selfish..." I shake my head not finishing the sentence because as much as I hate Tina she's Mia's Mom.

"Oh definitely." Mom's eyes narrow, no doubt remembering how Tina went out of her way to track my mom down and befriend her, all while she was having an affair with my dad. Tina pleads innocent all the time, when in fact she's a snake. "So tell me what's not sitting right?" That's my mom. She hates the woman, but yet she doesn't take the time to diss her.

"There's only a couple of people that knew about me and Mia. You, Dad, Tina, Martin, Barney, Lacey, Sarah and Jagger. There's no way anyone else could have known. Lacey's missing too so I'm taking her off the list. Sarah and the girls are like sisters, there's no way she has any part in this. So that leaves Dad, Tina, Martin, Barney, and Jagger."

Mum's eyes widen. "You never said me."

I laugh. "Do you really think I'd be sitting here talking to you about this if I thought it was you?"

She smiles, but it doesn't reach her eyes.

"What I don't understand is how they knew that Mia was going to be at her parent's old house?"

Mom frowns. "What?"

"Mia was staying at Dad's and Tina's. No one knew that she was planning on coming to Oakland... She left when Tina told her everything about me. It wasn't planned, so how did they know she'd be there? That's what I can't get my head around. How did they know she was going to be there? When I find that out, I'll be able to find out who has her." Right now though, my focus is on finding Juan. Once I've found him, my next job is finding Carina. Even if they don't know where Mia is, it gives me a chance to get them out of my fucking life. I don't trust them and that means they have to go. I wish I could do the same with Tina.

Mom's jaw clenches, now I know where I get it from. "I know why your gut's screaming. This smells like an inside job."

I nod, she now knows everything and she's jumped to the same conclusion I have. "The question I have is who's done it? Is it a known enemy or one that's yet to make their presence known?"

Mum shakes her head, tears swimming in her eyes

again. "I wish I could tell you that it's all in your head, that none of your men will ever betray you. The truth is Hudson, people want money and power and they'd do anything to get it. You have to think, who is desperate enough for the power that comes with bringing you down?" This is why I came to my mom. I value her perspective, she thinks logically.

I'm silent because the truth is that any of them could have done it.

"Do you think your dad has a hand in this?" Her voice is soft as if she's testing the waters.

"Honestly, he has the motive, but do I think he did it? No I don't."

"What about Jagger?" This time her voice is a little more confident.

My hands ball into fists at the thought of Jagger doing this. "He has too much to lose to do this."

Mom doesn't look convinced. "I've seen greater men fall. The real question is what are they getting out of doing this. Yes, they get the big acknowledgment that they made the big Hudson Brady fall. That takes a lot of balls. You don't just go up against your boss, up against a man who has proved his worth and take his woman. All that's going to get you is the death penalty, so why risk it?" It makes so much sense and yet it's just giving me more questions.

I have a lot to think about, the one thing I do know is I cannot trust anyone. Not yet; not until they prove themselves to me. I stand and Mom follows me, I feel guilty that I haven't visited her much. "Thanks Mom, I'm sorry for being an ass."

She smiles. "Since you've found love, Hudson, I've realized something. Your Dad doesn't define me, you are the reason I am here. You're the reason I wake up in the morning. I love you and I will do anything to protect you. I'm sorry that I've been a bad mom. I promise I will make it up to you and from now on you come first."

I shake my head. "No Mom, it's about time you put yourself first."

She smiles and nods as she places a kiss on my cheek. "Love you."

"Love you too, Mom, I'll call you later" I promise her and walk to Mia's car. There's so much to do and little time to do it.

TWO

Mia

"MIA, MIA?" Why is Lacey crying?

Opening my eyes, pain blasts through my head making me cry out in pain, I quickly close them again.

"Mia, are you okay?" she asks and I hear metal clinking. "Mia, will you please answer me?"

I open my eyes once again, the pain not as blinding as the last time. "I'm..." my voice is hoarse. Blinking, I glance around the room. For some reason I'm lying down. The dirty, off white walls are bare and the only light is coming from a tiny window. Looking over to Lacey, I see she's sitting on a dirty old mattress, there's blood just above her right eye. Licking my lips, I wince at the feeling of my cracked lips, along with the metallic taste of blood. "I'm okay, where are we?"

She shakes her head. "I have no idea." The terror in her voice is clear to hear and it makes me wonder what my voice sounds like. Do I sound just as terrified?

I try to sit up and cry out once again in pain along with a clinking sound. "Lacey?" I call out. My entire body is screaming with pain. "What happened?" Confusion sets in as I try and remember anything. I can't recall anything at all

"Don't move, Mia," Lacey tells me and I frown, why can't I move?

"Please, tell me what happened? Where are we and why am I in so much pain?" I cry as my heart races. I'm confused. I'm scared, and I just want to go home.

"Mia, I don't know where we are. I was at your house, waiting for you and these guys turned up. Mia, they tied me up and waited for you to arrive," her voice is shaky as she tells me.

"How are you so calm?" I ask her. "Who were they and how did they know I was coming?" I think back to what happened, only the girls knew I was going home. I never told anyone else. Hell, they were the only ones I spoke to since I left Mom and Harrison's house.

"Mia, I don't know but it's going to be okay," she reassures me. "You're okay," she says in a relieved whisper. "I thought they'd killed you when they hit you."

I shake my head, I can't wrap my mind around this, why is this happening? I grit my teeth and pull myself into a sitting position. The metal clinking has me glancing down, shit, I'm bound too. My wrist has a rusty metal shackle on it as does my foot. Great, there's no escaping even if we tried. My entire body protests but I manage to push through the pain. Now that I'm sitting up, I'm able to see this room much clearer, see things much clearer. We're both hurt, I hate to think of what I look like when I see Lacey's face. Her left eye is swollen, and her lip is split, blood running from the split down onto her chin. Tear stains run down her cheeks. "Who took us?"

Lacey shrugs, "I don't know Mia, I've never seen them

before. Although one of them did say that their boss will be happy knowing that he's got two of their girls. Whatever that means." Lacey says and begins to cough, spluttering everywhere as she does.

"Lace, you never said that you heard that." I frown as I take in her appearance, she's hunched over as she coughs. "Are you okay?" I ask but Lacey continues to cough, the sound rattling in her chest. "Lace, what's wrong?" Something doesn't sound right, she sounds like she's winded or something. Like she can't catch her breath.

The coughing continues for a couple more minutes, the sound ricocheting of the walls, making it sound a hell of a lot worse. "I'm okay, one of them punched me in my stomach and it hurt like hell, I've not really been able to stop coughing since. Hopefully, that was the last of it," she tells me, her voice hoarse, she's whispering, almost as if it hurts to talk.

"Let me know if it gets any worse," I tell her, not sure what I can do for her while I'm tied up.

"What do you think they meant that the boss would be happy?" she asks, and I shrug, I've no idea.

I close my eyes when it finally dawns on me. I remember what happened, Mom told me about Hudson, and I ran. I needed to get away, needed to clear my head and think. Tears trickle down my face. "It's us," I tell Lacey, I'm so fucking stupid, this is about payback. It has to be.

"What's us?" she asks confused. "Mia, what is it?"

I shake my head ignoring the pain that intensifies as I do. I was so stupid. I should have listened to her from the very beginning. I should have heeded her words. If I had, we wouldn't be in this position. "I'm so sorry Lace, I should have listened to you."

"What?" she shouts and the coughing begins again.

"Hudson." The tears begin to fall faster. "This is because of him."

"Oh shit," she mutters, her voice sounding hoarse. "How did you find out?"

"Mom told me Hudson is a drug dealer. He's like some big shot dealer. I don't really know, I don't really care. He's killed people, Lace!" I'm still so angry that my mom never told me. She knew that we were getting closer, why she let us get to the point where I loved him is beyond me. Surely if you love your kids, you'd want the best for them, you'd want them to be safe? That should have been the first thing she told me. But she didn't and now here we are.

Lacey's mouth opens in shock. "Are you sure?"

I nod. "You told me before I even knew who Hudson was. You told me that she'd heard things about him, that he wasn't a good man. I didn't believe you." I'm kicking myself now for not doing so. "I'm so sorry, Lace."

She shakes her head. "Don't Mia, don't apologize. He had us all fooled. Are you sure?"

"Mom and I had one of our conversations today," I begin and realize that they need to stop, they bring nothing but heartache. "She brought Hudson up, she told me he wasn't a good man. I was like you, I didn't believe it. But, it makes sense. The secretive phone calls. The way he'd change the subject if his business was brought up. The way he, Jagger, Martin, and Barney would all have secret meetings and then act as if they didn't."

"Mia, what did Hudson say to you once you found out about him?" Lacey asks, as she sits back against the dirty wall. Her lip has finally stopped bleeding.

"Nothing, I haven't spoken to him about it."

She gasps. "Oh Mia, why?"

I shrug. "He's lied to me Lace, I can't deal with the lies." I'm hurt, that's why. He should have told me.

"Would you be with him had he told you the truth?" Lace asks and I look at her, she really doesn't look good.

I think about it, if Hudson had told me what Mom had, would I be with him? Would I accept it? "I don't know. I don't think so."

"Okay, but surely you'd have asked him questions?" Lacey says and I feel as though I've made the wrong decision in not talking to him.

I frown. "Well yeah, I have so many questions swirling around my head that I want to ask him."

"Then why didn't you call him?" Lacey raises her head to look at me.

"Because I know he'd want to see me," I whisper and yawn. I'm getting tired, glancing at the window, I see that the sun is lowering. I have no idea what time it is. I'm trying my hardest not to move. Every time I move even a tiny bit, pain radiates throughout my body.

"And?"

"I'm not strong enough to say no to him. If I saw him, I'd be on my back and him inside of me within seconds." I tell her truthfully. "He's got this thing about him that I can't explain. Whenever I'm around him I feel safe, I feel as though I'm where I'm meant to be. It's like I'm drawn to him like a moth to a flame. I know that if I see him again, those questions I have will go out of my head and I'll be with him."

Lacey's eyes fill with sorrow. "You love him Mia, that's totally understandable. You're strong and I know you, you wouldn't just get back with him without resolving everything first."

"Maybe," I reply, but it's half-hearted. I really don't know what I'll be like.

"Mia, what are you going to do about Hudson when we get out of here?"

"If we ever get out of here," I groan.

"No, we're getting out of here," Lace says defiantly.

"You're so sure aren't you?" I'm not convinced.

"Well Hudson has said from the first day he saw you again that you're his. That means something, whether you want him or not, Hudson loves you and he's not going to let some asshole take you away from him."

My breath catches because she's right. Hudson's not going to let me just walk away willingly, not until I've spoken to him. He definitely won't let someone take me from him. "He's going to come for us." For the first time since I woke up in this room, I finally feel a tiny bit of hope.

"But how will they know where we are?" Lacey asks and I want to sigh, she was so determined that he'd find us and now she's wavering. "We don't even know who has us or where the hell we are, how do you expect Hudson to?"

"Have faith Lace, that's all that any of us can do. Believe that they'll find us." Even though my words are full of steel, I've lost the certainty I had only moments ago.

"I don't know if I have any faith left in this world," Lacey confesses.

"You spoke to Barney?" I ask, that's the only thing that I can think of that would have her doubting everything.

"Yes." Her voice taking an edge to it. "He called me while I was at home."

"What did he say?" If I ever get out of here, I'm going to have a serious talk with that asshole. What the hell is wrong with him?

Yawning, I bring my hand to my mouth to cover it, the sound of clinking metal makes me want to yell in frustration.

"He called me to see how I was." She shakes her head. "I thought it was so sweet and maybe he had regretted what happened after we had sex..." She trails off, her eyes fill with tears.

"But?" I ask, wanting to know what happened next.

"He wanted to know when I was back, that he'd love to see me again. I asked him about that night and if we were to ever have sex again would he do the same? He told me that if I didn't like it, that's my problem. That he doesn't do relationships and he doesn't do the whole after sex thing. He leaves, he always has and he always will."

Oh god, she really likes him and he's basically told her that he's never going to want her for anything other than sex.

"Lace..." My voice is full of sympathy and Lacey flinches. "He's not worth it. The tears, the sleepless nights. Lacey, you're more than sex, and you deserve to be treated like that too. Forget him, there's plenty of other men out there that will treat you with the respect you deserve."

A heavy sigh escapes her. "Why are men assholes? They either lie, cheat, or are complete jerks."

She's asking me something I'm dying to know too. I'm still reeling from the fact that Hudson hadn't told me what he did for a living. If he had, maybe we wouldn't be where we are right now. There's no need for the lies, lies only lead to heartache.

We sit in silence, both of us deep in our own thoughts. I don't know how much time passes, but darkness settles over the room. I'm terrified. Fear is choking me and all I want to do is cry but I know that's not going to help me, it's just going to make me feel shittier. My eyes begin to droop and I know that it's not going to be much longer until I fall asleep. Glancing over at Lacey, I can't really see her, I can make out her silhouette and see that she's lying down but other than that I'm blind. Gritting my teeth, I lie down, tears leak from my eyes as the pain gets too much. Once

I'm lying down, I release a harsh breath and close my eyes. It doesn't take long for me to fall into a painful sleep.

I wake with a start, I manage to catch the groan that was about to escape. I don't open my eyes as I'm not sure what's happening. My ears are filled with the soft snores that are coming from Lacey. I'm trying to wrack my brain to figure out what caused me to wake? Something must have happened? Other than Lacey snoring, I'm met with silence.

I try and get back to sleep but the snores are just loud enough to keep me awake. Damn. Opening my eyes, the room is still shrouded in darkness, I'm now lying on my back, maybe that's what woke me. The pain from moving from my side onto my back? Lying here I can tell that my pain is diminishing. I'm not as sore as I had been earlier. I manage to turn back onto my side without crying out in pain. Once I'm settled down onto my side, I close my eyes again and sink into the dirty mattress.

Keys jingling has my eyes popping open and my heart racing. That noise didn't come from inside of this room. When footsteps sound, I begin to panic. "Lace," I whisper shout, hoping that she'll wake up, but without alerting whoever it is coming that I'm awake, that we're awake.

"Huh?" Lacey says groggily.

"Ssh," I tell her still whispering. "Listen." And just as I finish saying the word, the sound of footsteps and keys jingle again.

"Mia," She gasps. "Who's that?"

"I don't know." I tell her as fear grips hold of me

"Someone's coming," Lace whispers as the footsteps are getting closer and there's nowhere for us to hide, we're sitting ducks. "Who is it?" She asks just as the door opens, my nose is filled with a musky vanilla scent. It's so strong that it's making my breath catch. I hate the smell of vanilla at the best of times but God, it smells as though he's bathed in it.

THREE

Hudson

SWEAT DRIPPING FROM MY TEMPLES, my knuckles pissing blood as I throw another jab at this fuckers jaw. "Where is she?" I ask him once more, my teeth clenched. I'm ready to snap this fuckers neck if he doesn't answer my damn question.

His face unrecognizable, I've done some serious damage to it but nothing too life threatening as of yet, the fucker smiles. "Someone took your girl?" he questions and I'm seriously losing my patience. "So that's the way to get to the great Hudson Brady?" He mocks me, "Alas, it wasn't me. Although I wish it was."

I shouldn't believe him, but I do and fuck me, that means every avenue has been looked into and nothing. Mia is gone and she's been gone three fucking days and I've no idea where to even start looking for her. My men have abandoned every job they were on and are out trying to locate her.

"And why the fuck should we believe you have nothing to do with this?" Jagger snaps his voice is cold.

Juan laughs. "Because up until this moment I had no

idea Mr Brady had a girl. If I did, she would have died as soon as I knew."

My feet move without me even realizing. My hands are around his throat squeezing the life out of him. Red heats his face as he struggles for breath, his fingers clawing at my wrists but I don't ease up, in fact I squeeze tighter. "I've always hated you, the worst thing my dad did was go into business with your sorry ass."

He struggles for breath, his fight leaving him, this is his last remaining moments on earth and I'm fucking glad that I'm going to be the last person he sees. My jaw clenching and my knuckles whiten with the pressure I have on his neck. "May you rot in hell you bastard," I say through clenched teeth as I release his throat and wrap my arm around his neck, snapping his neck in the process.

"Boss, do you really think he had nothing to do with this?" Jagger asks, his nostrils flaring as he cracks his knuckles. He's on edge. We both are; we just want the girls found. It's been three fucking days since the girls have been taken and I'm going out of my mind. Jagger is trying his fucking hardest to keep me from gutting everyone, but he knows it's only a matter of time before I crack.

I have no fucking idea who's taken them. I have an enemy out there and I have no idea who they are and that is what's killing me. Someone has a grudge against me and they've kept it fucking secret the whole time. It's my fault the girls are gone, it has to be. There's no other explanation for why they have been gone for three days and we've not heard one word about them. No proof of life, no phone call, no ransom demand, nothing. I'm going mad, I'm losing my sanity. Every second I don't hear anything, a piece of me dies. It's funny I didn't think I had a heart until having her in my life. It proved that I can love someone. Mia's everything and I'm not going to stop until I find her and whoever has got her is going to die by the most painful, slowest death I can think of. They're a dead man walking. You do not fuck with Hudson Brady, and if you do you face the consequences.

"Yes, I do believe he had nothing to do with this. The man was a psychopath, if he found out that I had a woman after me deporting his cousin, he would have killed her, there's no doubt about it. So yes, he had nothing to do with their disappearance." It fucking pains me to say that shit, it just proves that I have no idea where they are.

"What are you going to do?" Jag asks cracking his neck from side to side.

I stare at him. "We need to find who has them. Any ideas?" I ask, this is how bad it's got when I have to ask him for ideas because I have no idea who could have taken them.

"We start from the beginning," he tells me before he glances to the side. "Hudson, I hate to say it but I think we have a rat. Someone in our organization knows where the girls are. Someone has them."

I shake my head, this is something I've been battling with internally.

Jagger smirks, his pearly white teeth showing as he does so. "Yeah, I don't think so either but after all the shit that's happened; Juan finding out we had his cousin deported and someone finding out about Mia and Lacey." He shrugs. "There has to be rat. We've a snitch in the ranks."

"Jagger, if there's a snitch it points to five people, they're the only ones that know about Mia and Lacey. Those five people are my dad, Tina, Barney, Martin, and you. Do you really think my dad's going to be a snitch? Do you believe Tina would put her daughter in danger? Put Lacey in danger?" He shakes his head. "So that leaves three... You, Martin, and Barney. Which one is it?" I ask and his eyes widen, before anger fills them. "Yeah, you get what I'm talking about. There's a snitch and it's someone very, very close to us."

"Barney." He growls. "It has to be with everything that happened with Lacey. What is it, pay back?" The look on Jagger's face tells me that he's not even going to give Barney a chance to explain himself, he's going to go in all guns blazing.

"Give the man a chance to talk. It might not be him, Jag." I can't believe I'm the one being reasonable. "Yes, he did Lacey wrong but haven't we all treated a woman badly?" Jagger gives me a look, one that tells me that he hasn't. I scoff. "Yeah. Because you are a saint." I reply sarcastically. "Wasn't it you that kissed that bitch only hours after Sarah left your bed? Jag we're not good men, hell we've never claimed to be, but when it comes to our women we treat them with respect. We show them what they mean to us. It's taken us a while to get them back, we never got the chance to do that properly before they were snatched from us. We're not going to let that shit fly!" I growl, all my pent up anger is bubbling on the surface. I've been fighting it back, keeping myself in check because letting it loose won't help anyone. Especially not Mia.

"It's time to talk to Barney." I give Jagger a glare. "Just a talk Jag, he may not be the one." I laugh, fuck me, when did I turn into my father? Before this I would have flown off the deep end. I'd have knocked anyone who stood in my way out, and yet someone has taken my girl and I'm being diplomatic.

Jag huffs like a child. "Fine, we'll do it your way, Boss," he says as if he's humoring me. "But that fuck says one thing, I'm slitting his throat there and then."

I laugh. He's preaching to the choir. If Barney does say anything to make me doubt him in the slightest, I'll kill him myself. "For the past three days this city has realized who is in charge. People are quaking in their boots just like the old days. I'm not letting up, not until Mia is home. Until she's by my side. I don't care how many people I have to kill, I don't know how many people are involved in this. I don't care. Each and every single one of them is going to feel my wrath. You don't touch what belongs to me."

Jagger laughs, "Yeah boss this city has bled. They know who's in charge, no doubt about it. Shame that the people who have your girl don't know it. They're in for a world of hurt, and I'm looking forward to dishing it out."

"You're a sick fuck, Jag, but I like the way you think." I smile and nod my head toward the door. It's time to leave, time to talk to Barney. There's something about him that I've never fully trusted, but I can't say for sure if he's the one who's on this. However my gut is telling me that he isn't part of this. I can't explain it, my guts never wrong.

Walking out of the office, I notice Martin standing in the hall, his eyes glance between Jag and I. "Everything okay?" I ask.

"Nothing new to report, Boss," he responds. "Barney just called, he'll be here within the next hour."

I raise my brows. I don't believe in consequences, and this is one hell of a one, especially as Jag and I were just talking about him.

"Tina won't stay in Hidden Hills any more, she wants to be close to the action." He reaches into his pocket and takes out his cell.

"Action?" I growl. "Action? Like this is some sort of fucking movie."

He sighs. "You need to relax, I didn't mean anything by it. I just meant that she wants to be close to you so she'd know as soon as there was news. Barney said that she's spent the past three days in bed crying. Your dad has had enough and they're coming to stay here in San Francisco."

I nod. "Thanks for the update. Find Carina, I want her found. How one fucking woman can escape over twenty men is beyond me. Bring her to me by the end of the night." I walk past him and toward the exit, I need to make a phone call.

"Careful with her, Martin she bites." Jagger laughs as he follows behind me.

Climbing into my car, I wait for Jagger to get in. Turning on the engine, The Bluetooth takes a while to connect but as soon as it does I dial Barney.

"Boss." He answers immediately.

"Want to tell me why you're updating Martin and not me?" There's no mistaking the directness of my tone. I'm pissed and the threat that's keeping my anger locked up tight is starting to fray. Jagger looks at me, he knows that I'm on the edge of offing anyone who gets in my way.

"Boss…." His voice hesitant, "He called me. I told him that we were on our way. I'm twenty minutes away."

I hang up pissed that Martin has just lied to me. With each minute that passes, I'm beginning to doubt everyone. I know that it's not going to be long before I start doubting Jagger. One of my men is a rat and I'm going to find out who it is. Right now, my main focus is on finding Mia. Once I know that she's safe and at home, I'll then focus on dealing with anyone who is a rat or hasn't stood beside me while this shit has gone down and there's quite a few.

"Boss, what the fuck?" Jagger says, his voice vibrating with anger.

I put the car into drive and the engine revs. "That's what I'd like to know too." Pulling into the road, my foot presses on the gas, my hands tightening on the steering wheel. "Jag, I'm so close to offing everyone and starting over."

He laughs but I'm being serious. I don't trust anyone and I'd rather start off from the beginning. "Hudson, you can't do that." His tone full of humor, "but I agree, I don't trust any of those fucks, not anymore. I'm just fucking glad that Sarah and Allie are in New York."

"If this shit continues, I'll do it."

"Hudson, I'm your best friend, have been since we were kids. I know you, you're holding on but you're close to the edge." I turn to glare at him, what's he getting at? He rolls his eyes. "Look, what I'm saying is, whatever happens, I have your back. Whatever you need me to do, I'll do. Mia's yours and that means she is ours. We're going to get her back, Hudson."

This is why he's my right hand man, my best friend. The man would do anything for me and, in turn, Mia. My hands begin to shake, "Jag, all that I keep picturing is what he's doing to her. I can't stop it. Is she hurt? Then what's happened to her." I'm unable to keep the fear out of my voice.

"Hudson, we're going to find her and if she's hurt, we're going to rain a world of hurt on whoever has done it. I'll be there to dish out a few hits too." A smile forms on his face but I don't feel like smiling. Mia is in the hands of some bastard and right now I feel helpless.

"Tell me, Jag, who do you believe has Mia, honestly?" I ask, I have my suspicions but something will come to light and then I begin doubting what I think.

A heavy sigh escapes him. "I thought it was Barney."

"Thought? You don't think so anymore?"

"No, I don't think so anymore. Especially after that phone call with Barney. Something is not sitting right with me though, Hudson." He shakes his head. "I mean, why is

Martin lying? Why is Barney being so secretive? And why the hell has your dad not contacted you? Fuck, why has Tina not contacted you? The woman's daughter is missing and she hasn't called you to find out if there's any news. So yeah, I don't know if Barney is responsible. I don't think he is but then again I could be wrong. This is a fucked up situation, one that I can't wrap my head around."

He's right it is a fucked up situation, and trying to find out who has Mia is like trying to find a needle in a haystack. Nobody knows anything. Whoever has her, must have a lot of backing. Or they're keeping it very close to their chest. Meaning they don't trust anyone with this information. That's what I reckon has happened. That it's someone quiet and unassuming. I need to find out who can keep something so quiet, my men talk worse than gossipers in the salon getting their hair done. That's why my mind is fucked, I can't work out who it is, and all I can focus on is finding Mia. But for me to find her I have to know who it is. It's a vicious circle, one that is never going to end.

"I tell you one thing, Jag, I find it funny timing that Tina and Dad are coming back now. I mean Mia has been gone three days now and they've not been involved at all in trying to find her and all of a sudden they decide they want to find out what's happening. It doesn't sit right Jag." There's something about Tina I do not trust, fuck even my Dad's a piece of shit. The way they've gone about everything that's happened since Mia's been missing has proved to me that they don't care about their kids. They're both all about themselves.

"You'll find out in twenty minutes, Hudson, but you're right something has definitely happened. Why else would they be coming here? I feel as though we're out of the loop, and it isn't a great place to be. I guess when they get here you'll be having two conversations; one with your father and one with Barney

"Yep." I say popping the P, "and I won't be going easy on either of them. I don't give a fuck that he's blood, Mia is mine and the fact that she's missing and he's not done a single thing to help pisses me off. He's never going to change, he's still an asshole. Thing is, if it had been the other way round, even if I hadn't known who Mia was and Tina was missing. The fact that she's my dad's wife, that my dad loves her means that I would have moved heaven and earth to find her for him. " I don't know why I believed he was ever going to change? Stupid me, I should have known better. Mom was right, Dad only wants what's good for Dad, fuck what anyone else wants.

"I know you would, Hudson, I also know that if it was me in the position you are in, and it was Sarah that was missing, you'd you doing everything in your power to find her. We are going to find her. I can't promise you when, but I can promise you that we will find her."

"I'm going to start with Barney. You're right he's secretive and I want to know why. I want to know what the fuck is going on. If he doesn't have Mia and Lacey then why is he being so weird? Why is he taking secret phone calls? Why did he not ask to be swapped? I mean he slept with Lacey and yet he doesn't seem bothered that she's gone. That doesn't sit right with me. My men do not treat women with such disrespect, you sleep with a woman you treat her right, not the way Barney's gone about it. Lacey's different." I'm seething, Barney's in for a shock when I get to him.

"Yes, Lacey's different, she's family," Jagger says adamantly. "Hudson, you've got you and Mia who are like a love story, you both belong to each other, it's clear for everyone to see. Your parents are married to each other, then you have Sarah and Lacey who are Mia's sisters, and then you've got me and Barney. It's weird, Lace is a sweetheart, she really is and she doesn't deserve the shit that Barney has brought down on her. He too hasn't even asked if we have any news about where they are." He shakes his head in disbelief, his voice full of disapproval

"I get that you can sleep with a woman and realize she's not the one for you, but you still don't need to be an asshole about it. All I need is a couple of minutes with Barney and I'll find out exactly what's going on with him."

Jagger laughs, "A couple of minutes? I say you aren't even with him thirty seconds and he'll be bawling like a baby."

I smile and my foot pushes down on the gas pedal harder as I pray that the talk with Barney will give me some information.'

FOUR

Hudson

I SWIRL the amber liquor in my glass as I wait for the door to open. The television is off and I'm shrouded in darkness, everything that's happened over the last few days has been re-playing over mind as I wait for Barney, my dad, and Tina to walk in. Martin hasn't called and I'm taking it that he's not found Carina yet. Martin and Barney have been with me since the beginning, neither have motive as I've never done anything to them, yet both have had plenty of opportunity. They're both acting suspicious. Either that, or I'm losing the plot completely and taking everything they do and scrutinizing it.

One thing is for sure, one of my men has Mia. There's no doubt in my mind, not anymore. I've thought about it so much these past three days, and talking to Jagger I just cemented the fact that what I believed in the beginning is true. Now I know for sure, I need to find out how they knew where they were going to be. Mia never told anyone. The usual person I'd go to, to find this shit out would be Martin. That isn't going to happen, not when I suspect him. I need to find someone else who's good at hacking.

The door opens, the sound of heels clinking against my floor just as the light comes on flooding the room with brightness. "Jesus, Hudson, why are you sitting in darkness?" Tina asks and I turn to see her placing her hand on her chest like she's a rich socialite. She's certainly living up to the money my dad has. The fancy house, the spontaneous vacations, I think as I hold the purse strings now that shit's going to stop.

"It's my house, I can do whatever the hell I want. If I want to sit in darkness, I will. What are you doing here?" My tone clipped, they've not asked if they can stay here, they've just assumed, that's not going to work. I'm not putting up with them here.

"Son, where do you think we're going to go?" Dad's his usual abrupt self, thinking that because he's my dad he can do as he pleases. No, not after everything that has gone down these past few days. The fucker hasn't done anything to help me find Mia, he just sat in his fancy fucking house and waited.

"A hotel, motel, hell there's even a hostel. Take your pick." I tell him not even looking at him. "Barney," I say getting to my feet, "Follow me, we need to talk." I get up off the sofa and walk toward my office, footsteps sound behind me and I don't look behind me to see if he's following me. If he isn't, he'll regret it.

"He can't be serious?" Tina's shrill voice sets my teeth on edge. "Harrison, are you going to let him throw us out? Where are we supposed to stay?"

I don't bother turning, "I don't care. Anywhere but here. Now get the fuck out of my house." I know I'm being harsh, but they deserve it. Neither my dad nor Barney say a word. When I walk into my office I go behind my desk, taking a seat I switch on the light beside me. It only illuminates a little bit of my office but enough to see Barney's face. His eyes widen, although he sits up straight in the chair. His body language is saying he's confident, whereas his eyes are saying anything but.

"Do you know why you're here?" I keep my voice even, I'm not certain that he's the one just yet. He's done a few suspicious things, things that have got my mind spinning. He's got this time now to prove that he's not the man that has done this, if he has this is the last conversation he's ever going to have.

He shakes his head. "No boss, I don't."

I clasp my hands in front of me as I lean forward, keeping eye contact with him as I do. "Want to explain to me why you stayed in Hidden Hills instead of helping find Lacey?"

I watch with amusement as he grinds his jaw, he's thinking about what to say instead of spewing whatever he's thinking, no doubt it's to tell me to fuck off and mind my own damn business. But I'm the boss and he's being respectful.

"Honestly, Boss, I don't think I'm in the right frame of mind to be helping. I'd be more of a hindrance than anything else."

That's not what I thought he'd say. I hide my shock, my face is even. It's why I'm a fucking amazing poker player, I have no tell. "Why is that?"

He shakes his head. "How do you do it?"

"Do what?" I ask, I have no idea what the hell he's talking about.

"How are you so calm? Mia's gone and you're so..." He pauses and I glare at him. "You. It's like your acting as though it doesn't affect you, but it does. How do you do it?"

I raise my brow, "How do I do it?" I can't keep the contempt out of my voice. "Mia is my everything which means I will do everything in my power to make sure that she comes home. That's how I do it. That is my focus. That is my goal. I'm not standing around watching everybody else do it because at least she'll know that I fought for her."

I watch his eyes shut, he realizes he's fucked up.

"It's the least I can do, it's what I have to do. I don't understand why we're even having this discussion." I stare at him wondering what the hell he's thinking.

He sighs heavily. "But I have no idea what to do. I fucked up so badly with her. I never felt this way about anyone before until Lacey came along with her smart brain and smart mouth. Not to mention she's gorgeous, she makes my head spin. I had no idea how to play it. Boss, that's not me. I'm the ladies' man. I fuck them and leave. I've never felt bad about it, it's what I've always done."

I can't help but smirk. "You're so fucked." I laugh, now I understand why he's being acting so weird. He's in love.

He rolls his eyes at me. "Tell me something I don't know."

I nod. "Barney can I trust you?" Even as I ask him, I still don't know if I can.

He flinches, looking insulted. "Are you being for real right now, Boss?"

"Yes I'm being for real, now answer the damn fucking question!" I bite out as I glare at him.

"Of course you can trust me, Boss. I wouldn't be here if I wasn't loyal to you," he replies instantly. He doesn't blink, he doesn't move, hell he doesn't even show any emotion.

"I believe you," I tell him and watch as his entire body deflates. "If I find out you're lying to me, Barney. There is nowhere on this earth's surface that you can hide from me. Do you understand?"

He nods once. "I understand. Now, do you want to tell me the real reason I'm here?"

I'm impressed, although I'd never tell him that. "Okay, the real reason you're here is because I want answers. I am your boss that's not why you fear me, is it? You fear me because you've seen what I'm capable of. You have witnessed first-hand the things that I have done."

"Yes, I have seen what you've done, just as you've seen what I've done. We're in this world together, Boss, it's a fucked up world that we live in. We need trust, I have blind faith in you, and I respect you not just because you're the boss but because you're a friend. You're a man that I can rely on to have my back if and when I need it. And here you are asking if you can trust me? That right there shows disrespect."

It may be disrespectful that I don't trust him but if he's not the man, that will change and he'll have my absolute faith in him. No one, and I mean no one has that, and they won't, not until Mia is back in my arms. "What I tell you does not leave this room."

He sits up taller, adjusting his shirt as he does so. He gives me a short, sharp nod. "You have my word I will not say a thing."

"I have a rat in this organization."

His eyes widen at my admission.

"Yes, someone is betraying me, maybe more than just someone. I intend to find out who it is and until I do, everybody, and I mean everybody, is under suspicion." I'm letting him know that he is not the only person that is being scrutinized.

"Why do you believe there's a rat?"

"Somebody has taken Mia, someone has taken Lacey," I state the obvious. "Let me ask you, who knew about me and Mia?"

He frowns as if he doesn't understand the question. "I don't know, not many. You told us that Mia wasn't ready yet, I had no idea what it meant, but I let it be. It obviously meant that we weren't to say anything. Besides none of us should be saying anything. You're our boss, what you do is your business, no-one else's."

"You're right, no one else's business but mine and Mia's. How many people knew where Mia was going to when she left our parents' house?"

He frowns, yet again but he's not stupid, he'll understand soon enough. "I don't know, Boss. Who knew?"

"No one. Nobody knew where Mia was going. Even me. I didn't know she'd be there that day. Her and her mom had an argument. Mia fled and went to her father's house. Only my inner circle knew about Mia and I, nobody knew where she was going, so how did they know she was at her father's house? How did they know to take her?" I asked the question that's been plaguing my mind since that very first day when Mia was taken, it's only recently became clear that somebody in my crew has done this.

"Fuck," he whispers finally getting it. "Who? Who is stupid enough to do this?"

"That's what I'd like to know." Not knowing is making me go crazy, I feel completely useless.

"How are we going to find out?"

I give him a look. "We?"

He shakes his head as he tuts. "Yes we. We are going to find out who the fuck is the rat, we're going to find out where our girls are. Then we're going to make this sonofabitch pay."

Cracking my knuckles, I smile widely. "Yes, they're going to regret fucking me over. I do not and will not tolerate betrayal." There's an edge to my tone, he may have convinced me that he's not betraying me, but this is me giving him a warning. Don't ever do it, the outcome will never outweigh the motive.

"Do you have any idea who the snitch is?" he asks, his eyes twinkling with mischief. He and Jagger are the same, a hint of action and they're all over it, anything to get their hands bloody.

"I have no solid proof, all I have is suspicions."

He nods. "And those would be? Well besides being me that is." At least he can make fun of it. He understands that it wasn't anything personal.

I keep eye contact with him as I want to see what his reaction is when I tell him who I think it could be. "Right now, I'm very suspicious of Martin."

He sucks in a sharp breath, yeah he's shocked as shit. "Really? Martin? No, Boss I think you've got this wrong, too. I don't think he'd do this, he's not like the rest of us. He's too soft."

"Yes, I know that but with Martin all is not what meets the eye. There's something about him lately that just doesn't sit right. I want to know what it is." The last couple of weeks just little things have been nagging at me. The secret phone calls, the lies, and then to top it off there's now someone who's betraying me. It screams him, but like Barney said, he's not the type to do it.

"That may be so, Boss, but that could be just down to the fact that his mom's dying."

I frown. "Dying? Explain!" I demand. How the hell didn't I know about this before?

"Boss, she has cancer. This is her third bout, they say this time its incurable. She gets weaker by the day. That's why he's been so distant, so preoccupied." His voice low as he informs me.

"Why hasn't anything been said before?" Why is it only coming to light now?

He shrugs. "It wasn't for me to say. He didn't want anyone knowing just yet. I found out by accident, I overheard his phone call."

I'm silent as I process what I've just been told. I understand that he's pre-occupied but I'm not convinced he's not the one to do this shit. "I'm going to have to talk to him."

He stands. "Is there anything else?"

"Yes, I need you to..." The ringing of my cell stops me. Pulling my cell out my pocket, I see Jagger's name on the screen. "Jag?"

"Boss, I've found Carina."

"I thought you were talking to Sarah?" I ask, confusion setting in, I had sent Martin to find her, not Jagger.

"I was, but I got a call from her dad, she's turned up at her parents' house."

Anger bubbles up inside. "Okay, where are you now?"

He chuckles. "In your sitting room, Boss, I know that you wanted to know where she was."

Getting to my feet, I end the call. "You're coming with me. Jagger's waiting for us." Walking out of my office, I see that my dad and Tina have left and Jagger's standing by the door tossing his keys in the air. "Jag," I say, as I walk towards him.

His eyes glance behind me to Barney. "He good?" he murmurs so that only I can hear.

I open the front door as I speak to him. "For now. He's coming with us. Time to finally sort that bitch out." It's been a long time coming, she's pushed me too far. I have two questions for her. Does she have anything to do with Mia and Lacey being missing and I want to know why she was with Juan. How did she know about him?

"You're in the back." Jagger tells Barney, his tone full of

anger. He's not taking my word for it, he still thinks that Barney had something to do with this.

"Did he say why he's been such a jackass?" Jagger asks as we get into the car.

I bite back the smile as I hear Barney groan. "Well?" Jagger asks, starting the car.

"Fuck, you're a nosy fuck. I'm a chickenshit. Okay? I want to kill anyone I come in contact with. I fucked up with Lacey and I want her back safely so that I can rectify that." Barney admits.

Jagger glances at me, a look of relief in his eyes. "So he's a sap, not a rat."

I chuckle. "Sounds about right."

He stands. "Is there anything else?"

"What about Martin?" Jag asks, "I thought he would have found Carina, he's a good tracker."

I reach for my cell. "That's what I'm about to find out." I dial Martin's number and wait for him to answer.

"Boss." His voice hoarse, "It's not a great time."

"Martin." I say through gritted teeth, I don't give a fuck what time it is.

I hear him sigh heavily, "Boss..."

I cut him off. "Why haven't you found Carina?"

He sighs yet again. "Boss, it's my mom. I haven't had the time to find her."

"Why haven't you said anything?"

"I didn't want anyone to know," he admits quietly.

"How bad is it?" I glance at Jagger, he has a tight grip on the steering wheel.

"It's doubtful she'll make it through the night."

Christ. "Call me if you need me."

"Will do." His voice calm, much calmer than I would be. "And, thanks, Boss."

I end the call just as Jagger pulls up outside a townhouse. "What's up?"

My gut's still screaming. "His mom may not make it through the night."

He frowns looking confused. "Shit, what's wrong?"

"Cancer," Barney tells him. "She's had it a few times, just this time it's not curable."

"Fuck," Jagger mutters, saying what we're all thinking.

"Let's get Carina." I need to get ahead of this shit. I'm one step behind and it's time to get ahead.

FIVE

Mia
―――――

"LADIES," a deep voice calls out and I'm instantly awake.

My eyes pop open, but the room is still shrouded in darkness. I don't know how long we've been here, I lost track after ten days. The so called boss has yet to come by and I'm wondering if he's even real.

"Ladies, you're here for a reason, and only one reason," the deep voice says, it's a new voice, but one that I know. It's so familiar but I can't place where I know it from.

"Why is that?" Lacey asks, her voice is weak. Thankfully she's no longer coughing.

"Your men," he returns and I want to cry, I knew this had to do with Hudson, I just hoped that I was wrong.

"I don't have a man. I think you have the wrong people. You should just let us go. We don't know who you are or where we are. Please just let us go." She's lost all faith in us even getting out of here, we've not really spoken much the past couple of days. Both of us just retreating into ourselves.

A dark chuckle fills the air, "Oh Lacey, you're so naive."

Lace sucks in a deep breath, "How do you know my name?"

Another chuckle. "I know everything about you Lacey. I know absolutely everything." He laughs again. "I know that your men are trying to find you. Mia, Hudson has almost lost his damned mind trying to find out who has you. Poor Barney, he's like a puppy that's lost his bone. Mia, Mia, Mia…"

I blink. "What do you know about me?" I'm surprised I managed to keep the fear out of my voice.

He laughs. "Of course I know you. You've done the unthinkable, you've made Hudson Brady fall in love. You should see him now. He's tearing this city apart trying to find you. Shame it's never going to happen."

Hope sparks inside me for the first time in ages. Hudson's looking for me.

"What are you going to do to us?" Lacey asks, her voice cracking on the last word.

"You, nothing. You are collateral damage." My heart begins to race at his words.

"What are you going to do to Mia?" The fear in Lacey's voice is clear to hear and I'm wondering if I were to speak now would you be able to hear the fear in mine?

He chuckles again. "Well that would be telling now, wouldn't it?"

"Are you going to hurt me?" I whisper, my eyes fill with tears and I will them away, I don't want to cry.

"First, I'm going to see what you feel like." His voice is so menacing.

I frown. "What?" What the hell is he talking about?

His hand clamps around my leg, his fingers digging into my skin as he pulls me down the mattress toward him.

My eyes widen as I realize what he meant. "No!" I scream as I kick my foot out, but it's no use. His other hand grabs it, his grip is painful, and it feels as though he's hurting my bone, his fingers digging so hard into my skin. He's so strong. It's as though I'm a ragdoll, the way he continues to drag me down the bed by just my legs. I feel utterly useless, like there's nothing that I can do to stop this.

"What's going on? Mia? What are you doing to her?" Lacey screams, horror pouring out of her words.

I can't see what he's doing and it's so frustrating as I can't stop him. All I can do is feel what he's doing and it's a hundred times worse. It's as if someone's taking my sight and my other senses have heightened. I hate it. Something heavy holds my legs in place as he reaches for my pants and pulls them down, my panties coming down with them too. He pulls them off, leaving the bottom half of my body completely naked.

My entire body is frozen, I can't move, all I can think is please no. No, don't do this.

"Please, Mia, talk to me?" Lacey begs.

I can't, I'm frozen in place.

The sound of his belt buckle is followed by a horrified gasp. The crinkling of paper fills the air and tears begin to fall down my face. I have never felt as helpless as I do right in this moment. I know exactly what's going to happen and yet, I can't move, there's nothing I can do to stop it from happening.

"No, leave her alone you monster." Lacey cries, I can hear the tears in her voice.

"Please," I rasp, finally finding my voice. "Please don't do this to me." I beg, even to my own ears I can hear the horror in my voice.

But it's no use. He just laughs at me, probably wondering why I'm being so lifeless, just lying here for him. I'm literally frozen with fear, there's nothing I'd love to do more than get up and fight but, I'm physically unable.

He lifts my legs, holding onto my thighs. "You're a gorgeous woman Mia, from the first moment I saw you, I've wanted you but I couldn't have you. You're the boss' woman. That means you're off limits." He laughs. "Not anymore. Now, you're mine to do with as I please." He leers as he enters me in one quick movement.

"No!" I scream out in pain at the invasion. Tears stream down my face as he hums in pleasure. He's not listening to me, he withdraws and pushes back in, taking his pleasure as he violates me.

My tears are falling thick and fast. God, why, why me?

The room fills with his grunting along with the sound of our bodies slamming together.

"You like that huh?" He asks. "No wonder Hudson's gone gaga over you. Your pussy is fucking amazing." He growls and his lips descend on mine, pain hits me as his teeth clatter against my mouth while he roughly kisses me. I keep my lips closed, but that doesn't stop him. He's taking whatever he wants from me.

I close my eyes and turn away from him my mind drifting to my happy place. Ironically, the only happy place I can think of is being with the person who made me happiest. Hudson. The way he called me Princess. I'd love when he'd growl it. I never did find out why he called me that and I guess now I'll never know. I remember the look he'd always give me, like I walked on water, if anyone told him otherwise he'd call them a liar. I think back to the way he'd hold me close every time we were within touching distance. The love that he had for me, that he showed me even though he never said the words. When I think about it now, it was so clear to see, the way he cared for me, the way he looked at me. He loved me and I was stupid. I ran from him instead of talking to him. It's not Hudson's fault I'm here. It's mine. I was stupid, I didn't trust him and this is what I get in return.

His movements get frantic and relief washes over me, he's almost finished. Weird squeaky grunts fill the air as he moves quicker and I wish I could drown them out with something else but I don't dare to open my mouth to speak.

Thank God, this nightmare is almost over.

All that's running through my mind right now, is that I'm glad he put on a condom. I couldn't bear to think of what could happen if he didn't. He pushes into me again, his body shaking as he shoves his head in my neck. He orgasms, moaning loudly as he does. I bite my lip to stop the sob that's trying to escape as he lays on top of me.

His heaviness is making it hard for me to catch my breath. It's as if he's crushing my lungs, stopping all oxygen from flowing.

He pulls out of me and I cringe as he places a kiss on my cheek, almost like a kind gesture. "Thanks for that, Mia."

I hate him more than I have hated anyone in my life.

The mattress rises as he gets up off it.

Please leave and never come back. I beg silently.

"I'll be back later" he tells us and I swear I can hear a smirk in his voice.

My entire body begins to shake at the thought. I can't do this again.

His footsteps sound as he walks away, the door closes and is followed by the sound of the lock being locked.

"Mia?" Lacey's gentle voice is my undoing.

I sob, my body shaking as I do so.

"Oh Mia," she cries, and within seconds she begins to pray. I can hear the Our Father through my sobs. "Please

Hudson, find us before he comes back," she prays as she says "Amen."

I don't think we'll ever be found. Whoever the hell has us is so confident that Hudson will never find out who he is. My mind goes back to him saying that Hudson was his boss. Fear chokes me once again. If we ever did get out of here, it wouldn't be safe. Whoever it is works for Hudson, they'll always be around. I no longer have any hope.

We're going to die here. Whenever he's bored, he's going to kill us.

I'm looking forward to that day, if it means I'll never have to go through what I've just been through again.

I turn to my side and curl up into a ball. The room is filled with my sobs, and I realize that I'm still naked from the waist down.

SIX

Hudson

IT'S BEEN three days since Martin's mom passed away in her sleep. He's been quiet and off grid, which I get but at the same time, we're in the midst of a war and I can't have my men going dark. I've spoken to Martin once since that night and just like I did with Barney, I confronted him. His reaction was very much similar to Barney's. Betrayal. He denied it and has vowed to find out who is the one behind it.

"Boss, what are we going to do about Carina? She's been sitting in that crappy motel room for the past three days," Jagger asks coming into my office, a smile on his lips, he loves that she's being made to wait.

"I'll get around to her. The longer she's left waiting, left sweating, the quicker she'll talk. Besides, she's currently going cold turkey." I raise my brow at him, I expected more from Jag, I don't let my men do drugs and that should extend to their women.

A heavy sigh escapes him. "I know boss. I know. It's why I distanced myself from her." He shakes his head in disgust, "I can't believe I got caught up with her."

I refrain from saying I told you so, there was always something about that girl that set me on edge. "Have you spoken to Martin?"

A dark look comes into his eyes. "No, I haven't." He takes a step closer to me and takes a seat. "I know you spoke to him and I don't know what he said to you for you to look elsewhere. But, I'm not convinced, he is either part of this, or he knows something about it."

I roll my eyes, not this shit again. "I know you don't trust him, but you should trust me."

"I do trust you," he says instantly. "I just think you're blindsided with Mia gone."

"Blindsided?" I growl. "Of course I'm fucking blindsided. Someone took her, Jag, someone close to me took her." Do I believe Martin? That's a question for another day. I still don't trust him, nor do I trust Barney but they've both given me enough to give them a reprieve. "Leave Martin to me. Right now, I need to find her, every day she's gone, the more chance there is that I'm never going to see her alive."

"I know, Boss, we're going to find her. So what's the next plan of action?"

I already have it set in motion. I'm not telling anyone my plan right now. I have enlisted the help of someone indebted to me, someone outside of my organisation. I've set up a trap, I'm going to draw out the rat. I don't know how long it's going to take, but it is going to happen. I'm just curious how many rats are going to scurry out of the woodwork.

"Right now, we're going to have a long discussion with Carina's father." The widening of Jagger's eyes has me worried about this. I never thought the day would come where I'd question Jagger's loyalty. I'm not sure if push came to shove he'd do what I need him to do in regards to

Carina's family. They are a liability, I understand that she is their daughter, but at the same time, Hugo works for me. His loyalty is with me, allowing his daughter the access to drugs, show me that that loyalty is no longer there.

"May I ask why, Boss? What has her father done?"

I nod, he may ask. "Carina wasn't just using cocaine, she seemed to get her hands on whatever she could find," I inform him. I keep my eyes on him, wanting to see how much he knows. If he knew how bad she was, there will be hell to pay.

"I know that Boss, I know that she was an opportunist, anything and everything she could get a hold of, she'd take. Hell most of the time I'm not sure if she even knew what she was snorting or injecting. Soon as I found that out I let her go. She didn't like my ultimatum, she wasn't going to stop." He doesn't sound as hurt as he once was when it came to her.

"But what I've found out is that she is addicted to OxyContin." His eyes widen, yeah that's news to him. "You see Jag, I think I finally realized what she and Juan were doing together. Carina has been dealing, and I believe that she and Juan had plans to try and takeover my business." I find it funny seeing a drug dealer also be a user. Usually a dealer steers well clear of their merchandise. It's why my men steer clear, we've seen first-hand what our product does to people.

"She wouldn't be that stupid."

I chuckle. "She's not exactly the brightest spark. You know what users are like, Jag. Anything they can do to get money they'll do it. I don't care who they hurt in the process. They'd kill their grandmother if they needed."

"What's this got to do with Hugo?" He still hasn't realized what's been going on.

"Where do you think she was getting the Oxy from?" I

figured out that her father Hugo is her supplier for the Oxy, and if I'm right, he's also been supplying it to Juan for distribution.

He shakes his head. "What a moron."

That sums it up. "Let's go and see what Hugo has to say for himself." I get to my feet and do the button on my suit jacket up and exit my office. "Do you know where Dad and Tina stayed last night?"

"Boss, they stayed at Tina's old house."

I grit my teeth, the house that Mia was taken from. "Who the hell let them in there?" My men were supposed to be guarding it. No one in or out. So, who didn't listen to the orders I gave them?

Walking out of my office he gives me a sideways glance. "Lance did, Boss, he was your father's solider for years."

"Call Dylan, have him bring Lance to the warehouse."

I don't miss the sharp intake of breath nor the way he misses a step. I don't give a shit, I thought I got rid of this bullshit a long time ago. If you're not with me you're against me.

"On it, Boss," he tells me and begins to call Dylan,

Stepping out of the house, I call Barney. "Boss?"

"Barney, I have two meetings today. I should be back by six. Have my dad and Tina over at my house by then. Call Delores and get her to have dinner ready for the six of us, I need to have a conversation with the happy couple."

"Yes, Boss, may I ask why six?"

"You, Martin, and Jagger will be joining us." As they're my closest men, I want them near, besides with my plan set in motion, I'm not sure who the rat is and who will be outed so I'm keeping my friends close and if it turns out they're my enemies, well they'll be close too.

"I'll be there, Boss, and also make sure that your father

and Tina are there too. Is there any news?" It's the same question he asked every day, if I had anything he'd be one of the first to know. If I knew where Mia was I'd be there in a heartbeat with my men at my back.

"No news to report. I'll call you if I find anything." It's the same reply as always. I'm ramping up the interrogation on my men now too. I've found a new way of getting all the info I need. It's been working well so far. It's how I found out about Carina and the shit her dad was up to.

"Okay, Boss. Call me if you need me," he says and I end the call and get into the driver's side of the car just as Jagger gets into the passenger's side. "Dinner at mine tonight at six." I inform him and start the engine.

"Sounds good, I'm tired of junk food." He clips in his seat belt, the heat of his stare is strong, glancing at him, and I wait for him to spit it out. "Is it a test?" he asks, crossing his arms over his chest.

"Is what a test?"

"Having Dylan bring his dad to the warehouse. Don't you think he knows what that means?" He sounds incredulous, he really needs to realize that I'll do whatever it takes to have loyalty proven to me.

"I'm not going to do anything expect talk to the man. You need to relax a little."

"Hudson, they'll both believe you're going to do something to him. They could flee."

"Do you not think that I've thought of that already?" He must think I'm the moron. That I'm some fresh faced boss that doesn't know how things work. He's been with me since the beginning and now he's doubting me. "Want to tell me why you're questioning me? That's twice today, Jag." My tone has taken a dark edge. If it were anyone else who questioned me like Jagger has, they wouldn't have gotten a second chance to do it.

"Boss, I didn't mean to question you. I just..."

"You just what?" I growl, pissed, he's not only my man, he's my friend. He should know not to question me.

"Finding Mia is the most important thing for you right now. Everything else isn't even in your mind."

I clench my jaw as I try not to snap, I understand what he's saying, I don't agree with it. "Yes, getting Mia is the most important thing to me but that doesn't mean that I'm not here, that I'm not present and taking names of those who are fucking up. I'm seeing clearly, Jag and I've my eyes wide open. So I know what's going on, I know what's going to happen, what Dylan and Lance are thinking but at the same time, I don't give a shit."

"Okay." Is all that he replies. Seems as though he's learned to shut the hell up.

I stop the engine once I pull up outside Hugo's mansion. "Are you going to be okay in there, Jag?"

He gives me a sharp nod. "I'll be fine, Boss. Let's get this over and done with."

As soon as we get out of the car, the front door to the house opens. "Jagger?" The surprised soft voice of Mrs Mawson rings out.

"Yeah Mrs Mawson, it's me, Jagger. Is Hugo home?"

"Yes, Hugo is here, come in. Can I get you a drink?" She asks as we reach the front door, she holds it open for us to walk in.

"No thank you, Mrs Mawson, although I appreciate the offer." I reply wondering where the hell Carina came from, this woman seems sweet as fucking pie. She obviously knows who I am, who invites a man like me into their house for a drink?

Walking into this house it reminds me so much of my father's and Tina's, marble flooring grand staircase. This house screams money, as I step into the hall all I see are silver trinkets placed around the hall, one that catches my eye is the silver elephant. I understand why they're here, they're structured in such a way that you cannot miss them when you walk in. Having silver and gold things scattered around your house shows your wealth. It also shows me that Hugo is a liar, when he started working for me he was in debt. How's he managed to keep this house and all the things in it? Not to mention Mrs Mawson is wearing the same $4,000 Versace dress that I bought my mom for her birthday.

"Hugo darling, Jagger is here to see you," she calls out, her voice soft but you can hear the strain in it.

Heavy footsteps sound letting us know that Hugo is on his way. And his eyes widen as he takes in both Jagger and I. Yeah it's not a good thing having both of us here at the same time.

"A word, Hugo." I smile as I watch him swallow, his Adams apple bobbing up and down as he does so, the man is scared. Good. "Let's have your wife in on this conversation too." There's no way that she doesn't know what's been happening and if she doesn't, then she deserves to know the truth.

Jagger shifts slightly, the fucker really needs to work on his tells. I know he's not happy with me being here but he has to understand that he works for me and what I say goes. They may be the nicest people in the world but if they're stealing from me then they die.

"Of course, Mr Brady, follow me into the sitting room. Are you sure that I can't get you a drink?" Mrs Mawson asks, her hands shaking as she walks over to her husband.

"No thank you, Mrs Mawson, I do appreciate your hospitality though and I can assure you that we won't take up much of your time, I just have a few questions that need answering and then Jagger and I can be on our way," I tell her following behind them into the sitting room.

"Of course, is everything okay, Mr Brady? What has Carina done this time?" The sadness in her voice is clear to hear when she talks about her daughter.

"Yes, your daughter is partly the reason I'm here." I stay standing as the others take a seat. "Mrs Mawson, how much do you know about your daughter's addiction?"

She frowns. "To be honest, not much. Carina and I have a strained relationship, we have now for the past few years. She won't allow me to visit her."

I nod and glance at Hugo as I inform her of the depths of her daughters addiction. "Your daughter is addicted to OxyContin." Hugo doesn't blink, whereas his wife audibly gasps before breaking down and sobbing. "You knew that already though didn't you, Hugo."

The sobs stop. "What?" The betrayal in Mrs Mawson's voice is clear. "Hugo what is he talking about?"

"I have no idea." He lies.

"Mrs Mawson..." Jagger begins, glaring at Hugo.

"Victoria, please call me Victoria." She glances at me. "Both of you can. Please can you tell me what is going on?"

Jagger stands. "Victoria, it has come to our attention that your husband has been enabling your daughter's addiction."

"No I haven't." Hugo yells getting to his feet, but one look from Victoria has him rooted to the spot. "Vicky, listen to me..." he begins.

But she cuts him off. "No, you shut up," she spits at him. "Jagger, please continue."

"As I was saying, Hugo has been enabling her addiction. He's the one that's been prescribing her the pills." Jagger's tone is hard, as much as Carina is a bitch, he actually liked the girl and he blames her dad for making her the way she is.

Victoria's eyes fill with tears, disbelief written all over her face, she keeps shaking her head.

"Now Hugo, you have a choice. You can either tell the truth or your daughter dies," I tell him matter-of-factly. It doesn't matter if he tells me the truth or not, I still plan on killing her. She's done nothing but cause trouble and I don't give a fuck what Jagger says, if his woman and child come home Carina's not going to leave them alone. She's the jealous type and Jagger and Sarah have something she hasn't got. Allie, their daughter.

"Please Mr Brady, don't kill her," Victoria begs. "Hugo, you better answer his questions, if you don't, I'll kill you myself."

I smirk, damn, Mrs Mawson means business. "What were your plans with Juan?"

He doesn't ask who Juan is, there's no pretences, he just answers the damn question. "Carina's in debt, as are we. She came up with the idea of supplying drugs to Juan and in return making some money. Carina said she knew the business as she'd been around you both for so long. She knew where you kept your supplies."

I grind my teeth, they planned to steal from me. "Did you really think you were going to get away with it?"

"I'm sorry, I just needed the money. My daughter owes the Healy's money."

"So you thought stealing from me would be the best thing to do." I shake my head. What a fool.

"I'm so sorry." He begins to cry, he knows that he's fucked.

"One last question." He nods, "Where is Mia?"

"Who's Mia?" Victoria questions.

"I don't know who that is. I promise you. I don't." His body shaking as tears fall down his face.

"She's mine. Someone kidnapped her and I want her back." I growl as I take a step toward him.

He scurries backward like the coward he really is. "I don't know, I'm telling you the truth, I don't know who she is."

I nod believing him. "Victoria, you have a choice," I begin, "You can either get your shit together, get a bag and leave, never look back or you can stay here and end up the same way as your husband." This is her chance to escaping the man that turned their daughter into a drug addict, if she stays, they both die.

She walks up to Hugo, he sighs in relief, he thought she was going to leave him here with us. Before anyone says anything, she savagely slaps him across the face. The sound of her hand hitting his face bounces off the walls. "You deserve to die. I devoted twenty five years to you. For what? Debt? For you to fuck your mistress?"

His eyes widen, "Vicky..."

"No, you gave our daughter drugs. You deserve to die. I don't." She turns to face me, "Where do I go?"

I shrug. "Wherever you want Victoria. It's up to you." I reach into my back pocket and take out an envelope, handing it to her. "This will get you settled somewhere. Once you're there, give Jag a call and we'll get you set up with a bank account."

She clutches the envelope like it's her lifeline, I guess it really is. "Thank you."

"It's time to go," Jagger tells her and she rushes upstairs and within minutes she's back downstairs with a suitcase in hand. "Good luck Victoria," Jagger says and pulls her into his arms.

"Be safe, Jagger. Mr Brady, after everything you've

done for me I know that I shouldn't be asking you for anything, but I'm going to."

I roll my eyes already knowing what she's going to ask.

"Please don't hurt my baby, please give her a chance."

"What do you want me to do?" I raise my brow in question.

"Let her leave with me," she pleads.

"It's time to go, Victoria." Jagger gently nudges her.

She nods. "Okay, thank you. Please consider what I've said." She scurries out of the room without a backward glance.

"End him, it's time to talk to Carina," I tell Jagger and follow Victoria out of the house.

"Who's there?" Carina says and I can hear the fear in her voice. "Hello? I know you're there."

"Tell me Carina, did you honestly believe you'd get away with stealing from me?" I say standing in front of her. She can't see me as she's blindfolded.

She sighs in defeat. "I don't know, Juan said that if I helped him, then Jagger wouldn't hate me anymore. I love him and he hates me. I didn't know what else to do."

"Carina, you've been around my men, who's the rat?"

She stills. "Rat?"

My hands reach for the tie of the blindfold, she flinches. I ignore it and pull the blindfold off. "Yes, a rat. Someone in my organization is betraying me. Who?"

"What makes you think I know?" Her bravado is back in full force.

Grabbing her throat, I squeeze. "Don't test me Carina, you won't like the outcome."

She sighs. "I don't know, whoever it is, they're good. I haven't even heard any chatter about it. If the men don't know, then I can't help you."

Releasing her neck, I ask, "Who do you think it is?" She looks away not saying anything. I pull out my gun, my hand outstretched as I point it at her. "Last chance," I tell her as I cock it.

"Barney. I think its Barney. That man is too slick. He has an answer for everything."

I nod and squeeze the trigger...

SEVEN

Mia
───────

I'M awoken by a shrill scream. Opening my eyes I glance at Lacey, she's asleep. My entire body is shaking and I realize that it was me that screamed. I must have had a nightmare. The room is still in darkness. I don't know if it's still the same day or it's a new one. Time just seems to blur. I always seem to be awake when it's dark, either that or we're somewhere where there's no light at all except for a certain time of day. I know that we're in a basement but where could we be where there's not much light? It's hurting my head trying to figure it out, I don't have the energy to figure it out.

"Mia, are you awake?" Lacey asks, the clinking of the metal from her shackles fills the air as she turns on her mattress.

"Yeah I'm awake." My mind is so messed up right now, I don't know what day it is, what time it is, I couldn't even tell you how long I was asleep for.

"Are you okay?"

I bite back my retort of saying what do you think? Instead I lie. "I'm okay, are you not able to sleep?" I don't want to do this stupid small talk. No, I'm not okay, I don't believe that I'll ever be okay.

"Mia, talk to me. I can hear in your voice that you're not okay. I don't expect you to be. I heard what that monster did to you."

I close my eyes in pain. "No I'm not okay, Lace, the worst thing that could ever happen to me, happened. I don't know how I'm supposed to feel. All I want to do is cry but what's the point, it's happened and I'm scared that is going to happen again. He said he'll be back, Lacey. I just laid here and let it happen." My tears start to fall thick and fast again.

"Don't," she growls. "Don't you ever say that. You did not ask for it, you did not want it. He had no right doing what he did. Never ever think this was your fault. It's going to get better, I promise you it will."

"You really think so? Because I don't. If by some miracle, we manage to get out of here, how am I supposed to live? How am I supposed to move on, am I meant to act as if nothing happened? That I wasn't violated, that somebody didn't rape me?"

Her sobs fill the room. "I'll be with you every step of the way. No one said that you'll have to pretend it never happened. You don't have to be ashamed, it wasn't your fault and everyone will understand that, Mia. The worst thing you can do is hide, lock it away and let it fester inside of you. I will help you through this. I love you Mia."

I smile, it's good to have her with me. "I love you too, Lace, I don't know what I would do without you."

"You'd be fine. You're the strongest woman I know. When we get out of here, please tell me that you're going to see Hudson." Her voice is soft, but hopeful.

"He'll be my first stop. I want to talk to him, I owe him

that much. God, Lace. I miss him so much." He's the one thing that has kept me sane since I've been here. Every night that I close my eyes and images of what that monster did to me begin to play out in my mind. I push them back and think of Hudson. I think of the way he loves me and it helps.

"I know, Mia. I know you do. What about your mom, are you going to have a conversation with her?"

I sigh. "I guess I'll have to talk with her but I have no idea what to say to her. She hates Hudson, she doesn't want me to be with him, she's never once said anything good about him and I don't want to listen to it. Not anymore." I don't want to listen to it, I know now that Hudson doesn't like mom, but he never said anything bad about her even though he had every opportunity. It just showed me that he has more respect than she does. He respects me and the relationship that I have with her.

"What about you? Are you going to talk to Barney?" I ask, there's something about Barney that makes me think that he deserves another chance.

She's silent for a moment. "I don't know Mia, I want to see him, talk to him and see what he has to say. But at the same time, he's hurt me enough and I can't take another hit like he's given me already."

I feel for her, unlike Sarah and I, we've found our guys, they knew that we were the ones but Barney doesn't or if he does he's too afraid to admit it. "I guess the question you have to ask yourself is will you regret not talking to him if you get the chance? Do you love him?" I think she does, but she's never admitted it before.

She hums. "I think so, I wouldn't have slept with him if I didn't like him. But I think I kind of more than like him." She sighs. "I don't know, Mia, I've had enough heartache, I can't take anymore."

"Lace, if you never saw him again how would you feel?"

Before she answers the door to the room opens. My breath catches as it does. How did we not hear footsteps? How long had they been there? I pray that it's not the monster that's back. Footsteps sound as whoever it is moves into the room, I can't make them out, all I can see is their shadow. I hate this darkness.

"Ladies." That deep gravelly voice makes the hair on my neck stand up.

No…no….no. He's back. My entire body freezes and I'm transported back to the other night, the night when he raped me. I'm so still as I wait for whatever is yet to come.

"Leave her alone!" Lacey shouts, she still sounds like she's crying. "You've done enough, just leave her alone. Don't hurt us."

"I hate to disappoint you," he tells us and I'm pretty sure that he's toying with us. "That is no longer an option." His voice is full of anger. "Things have changed. You two are the bane of my existence."

I lick my lips, my body won't stop shaking. "What the hell does that mean?" I ask with a frown, my voice as shaky as my body.

"It means that this shit is done," he growls.

"Are we going home?" Lacey asks, sounding more hopeful than I've ever heard her before.

The sound of his laughter makes my blood run cold.

His laughter is followed by a rustling sound, like he's moving. "One of you will be getting out of here," he taunts.

"What?" I choke out, why would only one of us get out of here?

. . .

Bang.

My heart skips a beat as recognition hits me that was a gunshot. I don't hurt, I'm not hit. "Lace?" I croak. I'm met by his laughter." Oh my God. What did you do?" I cry. My ears are ringing from the loudness of the shot. "Lacey?" I call out but there's no answer. "Lace? Please, Lace, talk to me." I beg. "What did you do to her?"

A whimpering sound fills me with a bit of hope. Lacey's still alive.

"She was never part of the plan. She was collateral damage," he says cryptically.

"Why, what did Lacey ever do to you?" I can't believe he shot her. Lacey wouldn't harm a fly, and he shot her!

"Lacey isn't the problem, but she is my way out of this."

Lacey groans in pain and I move to get to her but my shackle stops me short. "I need to check on her," I cry pulling at the damn chain.

Something clinks against the floor. "Find the key and you can help her," he laughs.

Shock hits me, he's thrown the key on the floor. I need to find it and when I do, I can get to Lacey. My hand reaches out and I touch the cold tiled floor, my fingers stretching out as far as I can, searching the floor to find the key.

"Good luck Mia, by the looks of things Lacey doesn't have very long. Oh and Mia, if you manage to get out of here. Tell Hudson that this is a message."

My hand stills. "What's the message?"

"Tell Hudson, this is on him. He really needs to watch out who he fucks over."

Bang.

"No!" I cry out, as the sound of the gun shot ricochets around the room. "You're a monster, leave her alone." But my anger is only met with silence. He's gone.

Getting on my knees the shackle pulls tight against my skin, biting into the flesh but I ignore the pain and search for the key.

"Lacey, please listen to me. I'm going to get us out of here." Tears fall as I search, I try not to think of the filth that lies beneath my hands, and my goal is to find this key. "Lace, talk to me please," I beg.

"Mia," she whispers, pain lacing her voice. "Mia, are we really getting out of here?"

Panic rises in me at the sound of her voice. "Yes, we're going to get out of here," I promise her, but I'm not sure if I'll be able to. I'm finding it hard to find this key.

"Promise me that you'll talk to Hudson."

My eyes widen at her words. "Lacey!" She can't talk like that.

"Shh, Mia. Listen to me okay?" Her voice sounds so fragile. "You and Hudson, you belong together. He makes you happy and vice versa. Don't be stupid, talk to him but don't try and change him."

I frown. "Change him? Why would I want to change him? I love him just the way he is." My hand scrapes against something crusty. Shit, where the hell did he throw this key?

"If he said to you, *Mia, for you I'd give up everything. Change my ways. I'll be a model citizen*. What would you say?"

I don't even think about it. "God no, it is who he is and it's not fair for me to have him change who he is because I may not like the choices he makes."

She hums again, the sound so painful that it makes me grit my teeth. "That's good. Have you found the key yet?"

Tears sting my eyes and I will them back. "Not yet Lace, I'm going to find it."

"Its okay, Mia," she whispers. "I'm dying. I'm not leaving here alive. I know that and I know that you know it too."

I do but I don't want to believe it. My hands are searching as fast as they can, but so far I'm coming up empty. "Lace, don't talk like that. You have to have faith, we're going to get out of here."

"Lacey, don't stop talking." I beg her, knowing that if she does, she may not speak again.

My hand comes into contact with something metal and cold. "Oh God. Lacey I found it." I cry out but my happiness is met with silence. Picking the key up, "Lacey!" I yell and try and find the damn lock to this shackle. She's not answering me. "Lace, please Lace, talk to me." I cry as I place the key into the lock and unlock the shackle.

Taking the key I crawl off the mattress and over toward Lacey. She's so silent, it's scaring me. "Lace?" I ask, as I crawl onto her mattress, my hands reaching for her. "Lace?" I whisper as my hand grazes her face. She's not breathing.

Pulling her into my arms I hold her. "Love you Lace," I whisper as the tears fall down my face. Pain like no other hits me as I kiss her cheek. I sob as I hold her close to me, not wanting to let her go.

This is all my fault. She wouldn't have been here if I hadn't told her to meet me at the house, hell if I hadn't made her come with me to moms this summer.

EIGHT

Hudson

IT'S BEEN three weeks since Mia was taken. I've not been able to sleep properly. I'm not eating, I'm like a zombie. I've done what I promised, I've torn this city apart, and every criminal is on my shit list. I don't give a fuck if we had a deal going on, if you weren't helping me find my girl then you are part of the problem. I've gained a nickname amongst my men; I'm now the grim reaper. I don't give a shit if I have that name, it shows me that they know I mean business. The past three weeks, I've killed more men and women than my men have since I took the reins from my dad. It's about time we showed this city that we mean business and you do not mess with what is mine.

Dad and Tina are staying in my house, I came to the conclusion that if I'm going to get to the bottom of who the rat is then I'm going to need to have everyone close. Every day my mind changes. I was told it was Barney, and I believed it was him, now I'm not so sure. I thought it was Martin but his actions have said otherwise. It could be anyone and yet it could be everyone, the one thing is I'm not going to lie. I will find out who it is and when I do, they are going to die the most painless death ever.

Jagger is the only person besides me that knows that Carina is still alive. After I fired that shot, I told Jagger to clean up the mess and sent the rest of my boys home. Carina and her mom are currently in Texas, they have new identities. Carina has been warned, this is her last chance. She fucks up, there's no helping her. I will kill her. Her mum is determined to keep her on the straight and narrow, although that works out or not is yet to be seen. I did however instil the fear into her, she knows that I have men watching over her. There's no way she's got to step out of line and if she does she pay the price.

"Boss," Martin says entering my office without looking, a laptop in his hand, his eyes narrowed as he glances at his cell. His mom died two weeks ago and since then he's buried himself in trying to help me find Mia and Lacey.

"What is it, what have you found?" I question him. His sole focus is on Mia, so when he speaks I expect that he has found something that can lead me to her.

"A discrepancy Boss."

"What discrepancy?" I hate this shit, if you've found something, just say what it is. Trying to build up some anticipation is bullshit. I don't need anticipation, I need the truth and I need to find out what the fuck has been going on.

"Boss, its Barney. I've found discrepancies with his bank account."

I clench my fists. "Talk to me." Is there no one that I can trust?

Martin places his laptop down on my desk, he turns the screen so that I can see it. "He's had four deposits of fifty grand into his bank account over the past six months."

My jaw clenches. So much deception, my organization

needs a complete overhaul. "Where's the money coming from?"

"I haven't been able to find out, there's dummy corporations after dummy corporations. Whoever has sent him the money, they're good boss. So fucking good. I haven't been able to trace them."

"Right," I say through gritted teeth. "Jagger!" I yell, Barney is a dead man. He's played me, I'm a fool, I should have seen it.

The door opens and in walks Jagger, his eyes narrowed on Martin. He doesn't trust him, neither do I but right now, he has the only lead we have to find Mia. "Boss?"

"Get me Barney. I want that fucker and I want him now."

Jagger's eyes widen before he smirks. "My motherfucking pleasure. I'll call you when I have him for you, Boss. I can't guarantee that he'll not be harmed."

I shrug. "That fucker has had fifty grand deposited into his account four times in the last six months. Martin's just found out."

His jaw clenches, he knows what this means. Barney is the rat.

"Have Aaron go with you. He's dying to unleash some of his rage too."

Jagger nods. "The best thing is, we've got the upper hand, and he doesn't know we know about that yet so he won't see us coming." He glares at Martin as he leaves my office.

"He has a problem with me, I have no fucking idea why. Want to let me in on the secret?" Martin snaps at me, as soon as my office door closes.

"Best remember who you're talking to. Watch your tone, Martin."

His eyes shutter, losing all the heat he had in them. "Sorry, Boss" he says, sheepishly.

"Tell me about these dummy corporations. What information do you have on them?" I want everything on them.

He picks up his laptop and hands me a file. "I'm on it boss. I'll have everything to you by this evening."

"If they have properties, I want to know about it. Mia is somewhere in this goddamn city and I want to find her, so find me something!" I shout, I'm so fucking frustrated, but my frustration is because I can't help unless I find out some new information.

"As soon as I find out anything, so will you," he promises, walking out of my office and leaving me alone.

Picking up the file, I flick through it, sonofabitch. Surveillance images of Barney and a woman embracing. So all the shit that Barney has said is a load of bull. He doesn't give a shit about Lacey, why would he when he has another woman on the side?

Picking up my cell I call my dad. "Son?" He answers immediately, probably wondering why I'm calling.

"Dad, you at home?"

"Yes, is everything okay?" he replies instantly.

"I'm on my way home. I've got some information, but I need some advice." I'm not too proud to do that, if it helps me find out where Mia is, I'll do anything.

"Of course, anything you need."

Making my way out of my office, I tell him, "I'll be there soon."

Twenty minutes later and I'm walking into my house, coming to a stop when I see Tina standing the kitchen. She has not once asked how the search is going, if I've found anything out. All she's done is look at new houses so that she and dad have a place here. She bosses my men around like they're her slaves. The shit she does grates on my nerves, I'm close to snapping and when I do, I'm going to snap her neck.

"Son, I'm in here," Dad calls from my office. Glancing at my watch, I see that it's almost midnight. Yet another fucking night that there's no Mia.

"Dad, thanks for waiting up," I begin as I walk around the room to my chair. I turn on the laptop and wait for it to boot up.

"Hudson, what's wrong? What's happened?"

I log into my laptop and face Dad. "I assumed when Mia was taken that it was Juan that had orchestrated it, if it wasn't Juan then Carina had something to do with it. Especially after seeing a picture of the two of them looking rather cozy."

He raises his brow, this is more information than I have given him in a long time. "But it wasn't them."

I nod. "Nope, they had no idea about Mia. So that got me thinking, who knew about Mia? Not only that, who knew where Mia was heading that day?"

He frowns. "No one, Tina had only given her the keys to the house moments before the argument. So how did they know where she'd be?"

I give him a pointed look. "That's what I've been trying to figure out. See, Dad, there was only a handful of people that knew that Mia was mine and those people are in my inner circle."

Realization hits him. "You think one of your men betrayed you? That they have Mia and Lacey?"

"Yes, that's what I think. I've been trying to find out which one of my men has done this and I've come to realize that I don't trust any of them. I received some Intel today that Barney is the one who has been betraying me. He'll be dealt with."

Dad listens on intently. "Dad, I need to find out how they got to Mia."

"Hudson, do you really think that Barney has done this?" He too feels the betrayal.

"He's had four deposits of fifty thousand into his account in the past six months. He's not innocent, Dad, far fucking from it."

He shakes his hand in disbelief. "Shit, he's got to go, Son."

"Jagger and Aaron are getting him as we speak."

He nods. "So, what do you need from me?"

"I had Mia's car searched, I wanted to know if she was followed by having a tracker on her car. She didn't. So the only thing I can think of is that someone had her phone tapped. She spoke to Lacey, she had to have told her where to meet her as Lacey was at the house too. I need you to find out who tapped her phone."

"Okay, I'll have someone look into it. Someone outside of the men. They'll keep it on the down low so no one will find out."

"Thanks Dad, I appreciate that."

He waves his hand. "No thanks necessary. I'm your father, Hudson. I'll do anything for you and in turn Mia. Not just for you but for Tina too."

My lip curls in disgust at Tina's name.

"I know you don't like her and you have every reason. I've warned her that while we're here she will respect you."

Finally he understands how it's played. "Good."

"About Lacey. That's what I don't get. Barney really likes her, why would he have her kidnapped?"

I hand him the file that Martin left and Dad lets out a low whistle. "He's not playing around is he?"

"What the hell are you talking about?" I ask as I watch him stare at the pictures.

"Hudson, do you not know who this is?"

I roll my eyes. "Obviously not."

Dad shakes his head, almost as if he's disappointed. "Son, that's Tianna Mancini, she's the daughter of Cesare Mancini."

Fuck, so Barney's in with the Mancini Mafia, just what I fucking need. "I'm going to talk to him, find out what the hell he's doing with her." You don't just date the daughter of the mafia, you have to be inducted into the family. Approved by the head, approved by her dad. So I want to know what the fuck Barney is doing.

"Find out son, and find out soon." Dad implores. "The last thing you need is finding out that the Mancini's are involved, that's going to start a fucking war."

I stand. "I'm on it, Dad. If the Mancini's have anything to do with this, they'll regret it."

Dad also stands, he looks at me like I've never seen him do before, a soft expression on his face. "You need me, Son, just call. I'll be there."

I walk over to him. "Thanks Dad. I'm hoping we're getting close to finding Mia." I give his shoulder a squeeze.

He pulls me into his arms and tightens them around me. "You are, Son, I can feel it." He releases me and I him. "I'll get someone to find out who had her phone tapped. We're going to find out the truth and everyone involved is going to pay." His tone is fierce, he's finally being the man I had expected him to be, and I don't know what to make of the new attitude.

The sound of my cell ringing fills the air, my dad nods and leaves my office. Reaching for my cell, I see Jagger's name flashing on my screen. "Talk to me," I demand, hoping that he has some news.

"I found him, Boss. Meet us at the deli," he informs me and I can't help but smile, it didn't take him too long to find him, I'm impressed. Barney mustn't have known that he is a wanted man.

"I'm on my way." I end the call, finally ready to end this shit. I need Mia back. I never thought I'd have a weakness, that nobody could ever be defeated. That changed when Mia walked into my life, I truly realized what love was and I knew fear. The first time in my life I've felt fear but it also made me feel alive, knowing that I'd do what it took to make sure I got my girl back. That I'm deadliest when she's in trouble.

I walk past Dad and Tina and grab my keys out of my pocket as I reach the front door. "Have you found her?" The softness of Tina's voice has my hand pausing on the door handle.

I shouldn't turn but fuck, I do. When I look at her, all I see is pain. Maybe she's been hiding it, burying it? "I don't know yet. I've found some new Intel. I'm going to try and extract information. If I find anything I'll call," I tell her and just like that, her expression changes. Shaking my head I turn and leave, I've just been played, Tina doesn't give a shit, and she just does whatever she needs to do to get information. Maybe Jagger was right, my head's not in the game, if I continue with my bad judgment my men could die.

Getting into my car, I start it up and head for the deli. The deli is what we call the warehouse that Larson Butchers own, Jagger trying to be funny called it a deli with all the meats they had in here. The Larson brothers get paid handsomely for my use of their warehouse, it also keeps them out of trouble with gangs and shit. They know that the brothers work for me and in turn everyone keeps away from them. It's a win-win for us all.

A chill hits me as I walk into the warehouse, damn, I forgot how fucking cold they have it set in here. The muffled shouts lead me to where Jagger, Aaron, and Barney are. Aaron's standing against the wall with his arms crossed scowling at Barney. Jagger is sitting on a chair playing some fucking game on his cell phone, and Barney is tied up to a meat hook, wearing only his boxer shorts.

"Barney, sorry to keep you hanging around," I say and everyone's attention is on me, both Jagger and Aaron snicker like school boys. "Jag, untie his mouth. No one is around and I have some questions that need answering."

Jagger does as I ask and removes the gag from Barney's mouth. "What the hell is going on?" He spits as he glares at Jagger.

"You have information that I need." Barney flinches at my tone. Gone is the calm and collected Hudson. My tone is full of anger and rage. I'm ready to explode and fucking God help anyone on the receiving end of it.

"There's some mistake, why the hell am I tied up?" he asks as he wriggles trying to get out of the restraints.

"I'm the one asking questions, not you," I smirk. "Now, where do I begin?"

"Boss, you've got the wrong idea." He's such a fucking weasel.

"Oh and what idea do I have?"

He shakes his head. "Boss, you've got me tied up, whatever the reason - it's the wrong one." Fear radiating from every inch of him, I wouldn't be surprised if he pisses himself next.

I nod and a hint of relief shines in his eyes. "Do I? So, you didn't lie to me about Lacey? You didn't tell me that you practically loved her?"

He frowns. "I did, Boss." He's so confused right now, I'm about to educate him. "I do love her, Boss, you know that."

I nod yet again. "You do, do you? So want to explain to me why you've been seen with Tianna Mancini?"

His eyes widen. "What?" It's a whisper, he didn't think we knew about that. "Boss, you can't be serious?"

I take a step forward so that we're face to face. "I'm deadly serious. Tell me something Barney, why were you and Tianna embracing?"

"Boss, you have the wrong idea. Dante and Lisa got married and they had a baby shower last week." Lisa's his sister, I knew she was getting married but no idea to whom.

Jagger laughs. "You really want us to believe that your sister married Dante Mancini? The capo bastone?" Dante Mancini is Cesare Mancini's eldest son, he's the under boss. Once Cesare is dead Dante takes over.

"Yes, I'm fucking telling you, they're married and Lisa's pregnant."

"Say we believe you. Why has Cesare deposited two hundred grand into your account in the past six months?" He's silent and that tells me he's guilty. If you have nothing to hide, why say nothing? "I've had enough of the bullshit, I'm sick of the lies. It's time to be a man Barney. Own up to your shit."

He sighs. "Fine. The money isn't from Cesare, it's from Landon King. I did a job for him a couple of months back and he's finally paying."

Jagger glances at me. "Why is it Barney that you're doing business with someone else? You are my man. Mine," I growl, fucking Landon King is the youngest of the East Street Kings.

All that Barney can do is shrug.

"I'm investigating all the dummy corporations that link you and whoever else you're working with. If any of them have a link to where Mia is, Lisa's going to die."

He wriggles against his restraints even more. "They

won't boss. I promise you they won't. I haven't got Mia. I wouldn't do that. I owe you my life, you have my loyalty. I would never betray you." His voice full of terror.

"I don't trust you, Barney." I tell him and turn away. "Jagger you're with me."

"Aaron, get rid of him. I don't give a shit how you do it. When you're finished, tell the men that we're cleaning house. Anyone who even thinks of betraying Hudson, best have their funeral arrangements made." Jagger laughs, he's enjoying this shit. I should have him tested, I believe he's a psychopath, or is it a sociopath? "I'm driving, I hate it when you drive," he says once we're outside, and I throw him the keys.

"That's because you're scared, I'm surprised you've not crapped your pants a couple of times."

"You've got jokes, Boss," he laughs as he opens the car door. "One rat down…"

"Let's hope we weed out the others soon enough. It's time to clean house, Jag." I'm done, anyone steps out of line, and they're gone. I've been too lenient with that shit, it ends.

"We'll rebuild, the men you'll recruit will be better than before," he tells me as his cell begins to ring. He pulls it out of his pocket and answers it. Hitting speaker phone as he does. "You're on speaker, Boss is here too."

"Good," Martin says, "I've found something out. Boss, I think I've found where he's hidden her." There's something weird about his tone. Whatever the hell it is I can't place it.

Hope and anger course through my veins. "Where?" This could be it, I could finally have her in my arms again.

"Hunters Point." He sounds as though he's gloating. What the hell is going on?

Jagger nods. "We're twenty minutes out, but this time

of night, we'll be there in ten." He pushes his foot down on the gas and my head's thrown back into the headrest.

I close my eyes and take a deep breath, my leg is jumping like I'm some sort of addict.

"Boss, let me go in first, this could be a trap," Jagger implores.

"Not going to happen. Just make sure you're at my back." If it is a trap, I don't want Jagger in the firing line for me. I'll take down anyone who stands between me and Mia.

"Hard headed sonofabitch," he mutters, but I ignore him.

It doesn't even take us the ten minutes to get there. When we do, I see that Martin has enlisted the help of Matt, Lucas, and Tyler. "Boss, this house has a basement apartment attached to it," Martin tells me as I get out of the car, I notice that my men are fully equipped, guns in hands and ammo strapped to them.

"Jagger and I take the basement, the rest of you search the house. If you find them, don't approach, call me and I'll come."

My men all nod and Jagger and I strap up. "On my count," I say, as we approach the doors. "Three, two, one… Go." I yell and Jagger and Martin kick down the doors.

Walking down the steps to the basement, I hear sobbing. Hope sparks inside. Jagger taps my shoulder, he hears it too. Following that sound, we come to a doorway. The door is partly open, using my foot, I kick it open and hold my gun up high. My entire body on alert. I know that this could be a set up and I'm ready in case anyone is waiting for us.

The light flicks on and my heart sinks. Lying on one of the shitty fucking mattresses is Mia and Lacey. Mia has

Lacey in her arms, as she sobs. I can already tell that Lacey is dead. Blood has pooled underneath her, she's bled out. Anger seers through me as I take in Mia's appearance, she's not wearing any underwear. She's in a t-shirt and that's it. What the fuck happened?

"Mia?" I croak.

At the sound of my voice Mia's head rises, "You found me," she whispers, a smile playing on her lips before she lies back down and closes her eyes.

"Help me get them out of here, Jag," I yell and reach for Mia.

NINE

Hudson

"JAGGER, call dad and tell him to get me a doctor." I'm sitting in the back of my car, Mia on my lap as Jagger drives us away from that fucking shit place. I've had Ryan come and take forensics for me. I want to know everything about that place, who was there and where they are now. Ryan used to work for the police department but now works for me. Ryan is an asset to my organization and I'd be a fool to put him in a position that would have him face a moral dilemma. Him working the basement where Mia was kept is something that he had said from the moment he knew Mia was taken. He spoke to me and told me that he'd do whatever he could to help me find the men responsible for taking her from me.

"Boss, do you think we should bring her to the hospital?" Jagger's reeling, he too has seen the condition Mia is in, not to mention Lacey's body.

"Jag, I don't know what the fuck to do right now. She needs a doctor, one that can deal with her properly. Mamford is out of fucking town, it's his wedding anniversary and he and the wife have gone to fucking Cancun."

Once I know Mia's okay. Hell is going to be paid. Barney didn't act alone, that much is true, I need to find out who he was working with.

"Boss, do you think she's been…" he trails off, "She's not wearing any pants."

Pain slashes me as the thought, I pull her closer to me and feel her chest as I have done every couple of minutes since we got into this car. She passed out as soon as she said I'd found her, I've not been able to wake her since. "I fucking hope not, Jag." If she's been raped, I'll lose my damn mind. I don't think I'll be able to take it. Just the mere thought of someone doing it to her makes me want to throw up and then kill them.

"Call Dad," I beg him. I'm so fucking out of my depth here.

The sound of his cell ringing fills the car, my dad answers after the first few rings. "Jagger, is everything okay?" There's hope in dad's voice along with anguish.

"Harrison, we've found her." Jagger's voice is tight, he, like me, is barely holding on right now.

"Is she okay?"

"We need to get her to a doctor, Hudson's asked me to have you organize it." That's technically not what I said but it's good, at least I don't sound like I've no idea what to do.

"On it, I'll call you with a location," Dad instructs and relief washes through me, she's going to be okay.

I place a kiss against her forehead, as I pull her closer to me. It's good to have her back in my arms but not like this, she's been gone too long, she's not been looked after, I feel the bones in her body protruding through her skin. "Love you, Mia, I promise you, nothing like this is ever going to happen to you again." I won't let anything like this happen to her again. No way, not ever.

"Hudson," Jagger's voice is soft. Looking up at the mirror, I see a tear falling down his face. "Why would they kill Lacey? It doesn't make sense."

I nod. "I know Jag, I know. None of this makes sense and I promise you, I'm going to find out the truth."

"Good, I can't believe that Barney had her killed. Why fucking sleep with her if that was the end game?"

Yeah, I'm not buying it either. "Maybe we got it wrong? What if everything Barney said was the truth? What if someone is setting him up?"

Silence fills the car. "Who would go to those extreme lengths? Boss, you saw the money in his account, the money lead us to Mia."

"It was too easy." Way too easy in the end.

I watch as he frowns. "Too easy? How did you work that out?"

"Jag, there was no one at the house, either in the main house or basement other than Mia and Lacey. Why is that? If they were holding them for a reason why were there no guards? Why was the door open for Mia to walk out if she so wanted?" Nothing is making sense right now and until Mia can help us connect the dots, we're stuck in limbo, going round in circles trying to make sense of this.

"And she what? Decided to stay there instead of walking out of the door? Hudson, I think we got the right man."

I shake my head, I don't. "Call Aaron," I instruct him, I want to have Aaron check into what Barney was saying.

He sighs but does as I ask, and set his cell calling. "Jag?"

"Aaron, I need you to do something for me," I say loud enough so that I can be heard from the backseat. "It needs to be done discreetly, only Jagger and I are to know about this. You do not say a word to anyone. You do, you die." It's that simple.

He doesn't even hesitate. "What do you need, Boss?"

"Find out if what Barney told us was correct. I want to know why he was with Tianna." I'll call Landon once I get Mia to a doctor.

"On it boss. I won't say anything to anyone. If I'm asked, I'll say that I'm given some personal time while Mia is recuperating."

I smile. "Good, I'll talk to you soon, Aaron."

"Boss," he says quickly so that Jagger doesn't end the call. "How is Mia?"

"I don't know Aaron, I'll find out once I get her to a doctor." I need Dad to hurry the hell up and call with a location.

"Okay boss, keep me informed. My prayers are with you both. I'll call when I find out any information."

"Thanks Aaron and I will do," I tell him and Jagger ends the call. "Fuck, when the hell is Dad going to call?" I'm ready to go to the damn hospital. Mia needs medical attention and I'll deal with the fall out.

"He'll call, Hudson, you know he will," Jagger says calmly and I know I should be too, but right now, with Mia unconscious in my arms, calm has gone out the window and fear has a grip of me. "Hudson, you have her back, that is the main thing. She's going to be okay."

My jaw clenches as my eyes close. I lean into Mia and inhale deeply, he's right; I do have her back but I think he's wrong, I don't believe that she's going to be okay. She was there when Lacey died, the dried blood on her top is a testament to how she tried to help her. If it were me and Jagger was killed, I'd go on a rampage, but this is Mia we're talking about. She's good and pure, nothing evil was meant to have touched her.

Jagger's cell rings and I wait with bated breath as he answers. "Jagger, get Mia to 128 Texas Street. A doctor will be there in minutes. She'll make sure Mia is well looked after."

"On it," Jagger responds as he glances in his side mirror and does a U-turn, the wheels spinning as he does so. "We'll be there in less than five minutes."

"Hear that, Mia? We'll see the doctor in five minutes. You'll be okay," I tell her, even though I'm not sure if she can hear me or not.

She's still breathing but it's very faint. "Love you, Mia," I whisper into her hair.

"We're here, Boss," Jagger says as he comes to a screeching halt outside a house. Thank fuck.

Jagger's out of the car and around to the back in seconds, as soon as he opens the door, he helps me get Mia out of the car. Gingerly holding her in his arms as I climb out. Hushed whispers get my attention, peering across the street, I see my men forming a line. They want to know what's happened. They'll have to wait. "Jag, fill them in on what's happened. I'll let them know how Mia is once I know myself."

He nods handing me Mia, "I will do, Boss." His eyes are on Mia's fragile frame, she's not once moved since I picked her up off that shitty mattress.

As soon as I enter the little house, Mia's immediately taken from me by a couple of nurses and brought into one of the rooms. "Mr Brady, I'm Dr Erika Telemann. I'll be looking after Mia. I'll keep you informed when I know anything." Erika gives me a small smile before following the nurses and Mia into another room.

I lean against the wall and bow my head as relief crashes through me, she's in safe hands, I can finally breathe again.

"Son," Dad's low hesitant tone makes my head lift. His hands in his pockets but his eyes are focused on me. I've never seen my dad look so uncomfortable before. "How is she?"

I shrug. "I have no fucking idea, Dad. The doctor's with her now. I don't know where you managed to get her from, but I'm grateful."

He waves it away as if it were nothing. "Is there anything I can do?"

"Right now, there's nothing anyone can do. She's unconscious and I won't know what happened until she wakes up. God knows when that'll be." My voice is hoarse as I try and fight back the tears that are threatening to fall.

"What about Lacey? Can she tell us anything?"

Pain hits me and I rub my chest as if that's going to help. "She's dead, Dad. We got there too late. Mia was cradling Lacey's body."

His eyes widen. "Fuck," he bites out.

I nod. "Where's Tina?" I thought she'd be here.

He sighs. "She's at home, I haven't told her we've found her yet."

I hide my shock. "And why is that?"

He looks away, almost if he's ashamed. "I've made a lot of mistakes in my life, Hudson, most of them involve you and how I was. Since Tina met you, things between us have gone downhill. She's not the woman I married," he admits and I know how hard it is for him to say that he's got anything wrong. "The way she's acted since Mia was taken just hasn't sat right with me."

At least I'm not the only one. "When will you be getting the information?"

He raises his eyebrow but laughs. "Nothing can ever get past you. I had Galen look into her a bit more thoroughly than the last time. I've also had him look into all the men. Someone's a rat and I want to find out who it is."

"You don't think it was Barney?" I question, I want to see if anyone else thinks the same as I do.

He shrugs. "I don't know, what has he said?"

"He got the money for doing a job for Landon King and Landon's been paying him sporadically. He met Tianna at his sister's baby shower. Lisa married Dante Mancini." Even as I say the words, it sounds far-fetched but why would he lie about something that is so easily confirmed?

"Wait… Dante married Barney's sister?" Disbelief in his words.

"Apparently. Hell, I didn't even know he got married."

Dad laughs. "It was an arranged marriage, one that was meant to help bring two families together."

"That makes no fucking sense, Dad. Barney wasn't Mafia." I know that for a fact, there's no way, no how.

"No, Son, he wasn't but Lisa has a different dad. Lisa's mom ran off with Lisa when she found out the truth about her father. It took Orlando and his men almost fifteen years to find her, by that time Lisa's mom had remarried and had another child… Barney. When Barney's mom died before they reached eighteen, Orlando took Lisa in and has groomed her to marry."

I shake my head, its political bullshit. I know what I need to know and that's enough for me, the ins and outs of how the Mafia handle their family is something I want no part in. I do my business and if that leads me to come in contact with anyone, I'll find shit out then. "So? It's true? Lisa married Dante?"

He nods. "I didn't know Lisa as Barney's sister, I only knew her as Lisa Russo. The daughter of Orlando Russo."

This shit gets weirder by the second. "If that's the case, why didn't Barney go and be a solider for Orlando?"

Dad gives me a smile. "Because of you, Son. You're the reason he joined my ranks. He was in awe of you. You were what he aspired to be. He told me that if he could emulate even a fifth of you, he'd be a happy man. I think he was just sick of being a nobody, when his sister was a Principessa. He believed that joining me would help him. He made friends and became a man that was well respected."

"He's dead, Dad. He lied to me too many times," I tell him matter-of-factly. I will not be made feel guilty for killing him. He lied time and time again to me. It was only a matter of time before those lies caught up to him.

Dad nods. "I know Son, you did the right thing. Everyone knows that."

"I find it weird that there was no one in the basement when we found Mia. Not only that, the basement door was open and the shackles were off Mia but not Lacey. Mia could have ran, she had the chance."

"Are you saying you think Mia stayed there by choice?" He looks disgusted at the thought.

"I know she did, Dad and it wasn't anything like you're thinking. She stayed with Lacey." She stayed with her friend, the woman she considers her sister.

Dad frowns. "Okay, so what do you find weird then?"

I roll my eyes. "No one was there. It was like they knew we were coming."

Realization hits him. "How many people knew you were going to be there?"

"Six of us. That's all. Matt, Lucas, Tyler, Martin, Jagger, and myself."

"You've narrowed it down. One of those five is the

man that is betraying you," Dad tells me something I already had figured out.

"And I'm going to find out who and when I do…"

The door behind me opens and I turn and see Dr Erika walking out, her face blank. I can't decipher if she has good or bad news. "Mr Brady, may I have a word in private?" she asks softly and I fear the worse already.

"I'll step outside," Dad says, but I shake my head and he stays standing where he is.

"Its okay, Doc, this is my dad."

She nods once and takes a deep breath. "Mr Brady, Mia has a lot of bruising, mainly to her face. She has a contusion on her head, we're monitoring it, it's no longer bleeding and has been stitched but the blow has broken her eye socket. She's got a broken nose, but all those will heal in time. She doesn't appear to have any serious injuries. Right now her body is healing, that's why she's unconscious. She'll wake once she's ready."

"But?" I can hear it in her voice, something else is wrong.

She shifts from side to side, her eyes glancing from me to my father.

"Tell me," I say through clenched teeth.

"Mr Brady, Mia has been sexually assaulted."

"Who?"

She frowns. "Excuse me?"

"Who raped her?" I spit out, whoever did it is going to hurt. I'm going to ruin them. They're going to wish they had never heard of Hudson Brady by the time I'm finished with them.

She splutters. "Mr Brady, I'm sorry but I have no way of knowing that. I've taken a rape kit…."

"Give it to me," I demand, holding out my hand.

Her eyes widen. "Mr Brady, that kit has to go to the

police. If you give it to them, they will find the person responsible for this."

"Doc, I know that you think that's the best thing to do. But let me tell you this. When I find out who did this, I'm going to make sure they never do it to anyone else. I'm going to make them hurt so bad, they'll be begging for forgiveness. They'll be begging for the end."

She looks away, I can see the internal war that she's having with herself.

"Doc, no one knows we're here. So no one is going to know that you took that kit and gave it to me."

She gives me a sharp nod and turns back and walks into Mia's room.

"Son, what's your plan of action now?" Dad asks when we're alone.

"My gut is screaming that it's one of those five we spoke about. One of them raped Mia and I'm going to find out who."

Dad nods. "I'll take the kit and have it ran by someone outside of your men."

I agree. "I don't know how deep this deception runs, who else they have helping them." At least there are a few that I know aren't involved in this shit, but are they helping them? That's what I don't know.

"I'll get on it right away. I'll tell them to put a rush on it." His eyes flashing with rage.

"What about DNA?" I ball my fists up, I don't want my dad seeing them shaking.

"That's where you're going to have to get creative. We're going to need a sample from each of them."

I smirk. "Once we do, I'm going to nail the bastard who orchestrated this." I've never felt so much rage as I do now. God help the fucker, because when I'm finished with him, he'll be unrecognizable.

"Are you going to tell anyone what's happened to Mia?" Dad asks softly. It's a vast change from the anger it held moments ago.

I shake my head. "No, until Mia is awake, no one is to know anything."

"Okay son, I won't say a word." He promises as Dr Erika steps out of the room, a bag in her hand. "I'll take that," Dad tells her and she immediately hands it to him before going back into Mia's room, not once talking. "Son, call me if she wakes."

"I will do. Thanks Dad. I owe you."

He shakes his head. "Nothing to owe. She's yours which means she's mine." He places his hand on my shoulder and squeezes tightly.

I hear the door closing, and I know he's just left. He's going to find out who did this. I take a seat and wait until the good doctor says I can see Mia.

TEN

Mia
———

I WAKE up to hushed tones. Fear immediately grips me. I can't open my eyes, I try but it's to no avail. I don't know who's here. Is it him? Is he back? I inhale, but I don't get the dirty waft that I had while I was in that room, instead, the scent of lavender and cleaning chemicals fill my nose. Where am I? Where's Lacey? She's not beside me anymore.

"How is she?" That soft dulcet tone makes me feel at ease. "Her face looks bad." The southern drawl he has takes a hardness to it.

"The doc says she's going to be okay." Relief washes through me when I hear Hudson's voice. "But fuck, she's been through a lot. I don't know if she ever will be."

"She's strong and she has you too," Jagger tells him, it's something that I love about Jagger, he always has something to say that's uplifting.

"She left, remember? She found out who I was and she ran." The disappointment in his voice makes me want to cry. Lacey was right, I should have spoken to him first instead of running. I just didn't know how to deal with it. I try and move my fingers but I can't, I'm so tired but I don't want to fall asleep again. I want to listen to Hudson. Hearing his voice is making me feel safe. I want to listen to it forever. It means I'm not back in that place.

"You'll never know unless you talk to her. Sarah keeps texting, wanting to know if she's awake. She wants to come home but I've told her she's staying put. I'm sending Ma to New York to spend time with her. At least until this fucking asshole is found. I can't have her or Allie in this."

"Sarah's going to love that…" I can hear the smile in Hudson's voice.

"I know, my ma's going to make Sarah want me or she's going to send her running for the hills. I'm not sure which yet. Look Hudson, I know something has happened. The way that your father is behaving, the secret phone calls. What is it?" Jagger sounds really worried. He's usually so light hearted, what has happened.

A heavy sigh escapes him. "Jag, I have no idea who the hell I can trust."

"You don't think you can trust me?" The accusation is clear, the anger is there.

"I don't know, Jag. I fucking don't know." Hudson tells him sounding resigned.

"You should know that you can trust me. How long have we been friends?"

"Jag, someone close to me kidnapped Mia. They fucking took her for over three fucking weeks. They knew where she was going to be and I need to find out how. There was only five people who knew that Jag, five. So no I don't know who to trust right now."

"You should fucking trust me! Christ, Hudson, do you really think I would have done this? She's your woman, Hudson that means she's family. She's Sarah's best friend, she's made sure that my woman and my baby girl have been okay. I wouldn't do anything to hurt her. Ever." The anger that Jagger has is understandable, hell even I'm mad that Hudson thinks he can't trust Jagger.

"He raped her, Jag, the man that took the woman I love. Raped her."

My breath catches at his words. I never wanted him to find out, I never wanted anyone to find out. I truly believed that when Lacey died no one would ever know. But he does and I honestly don't know how to react to that news.

"Fuck, Hudson." It's a guttural sound, one that reminds me of a wild animal that's been cornered.

"So, while I appreciate the doc saying she's going to be okay. I don't think she will be. Someone close to me did this to her. They assaulted her in every way possible, they killed her best friend in front of her and kept her in a fucking basement like a damned animal."

"I know that you're going to do whatever it takes to make her safe. Whatever that may be. Trust me, Hudson, I've never betrayed you and I never would. You're my brother and it fucking hurts that you even thought it could be me. I know that you've got your father working on this but I am too. I'm going to find out who did this to you, to Mia."

I hear movement followed by a door closing. My lips part and I try and say his name, "Hudson." It comes out hoarse, my eyes still can't open, and as I try my entire body is protesting against it.

"Fuck." His curse is followed by a chair scrapping against the floor. "Mia, fuck."

I lick my lips. "Hudson. Where am I?"

Hands roam my face and I move from the touch, crying out in pain as I do.

His hands immediately leave my face. "Mia, it's me. You're safe." Hurt in his voice.

"Where I am?" I ask again feeling awful for pulling away from him.

"You're in a safe house, the doctor has been and she's made sure you're okay."

"Why can't I open my eyes?" I still can't open them.

"Mia, you were hit in the face. It was a severe blow that you took. It's broken your eye socket. Not only that, the fucker broke your nose. Your eyes are swollen."

"How bad does it look?" I ask, imagining the worst. "What else happened?" I can't remember much after crawling onto the mattress beside Lacey. My heart hurts thinking about her, it's my fault that she's dead. If I had just called Hudson when I found out who he really is, this wouldn't have happened.

"You look gorgeous as always. Mia, Lacey died, you were…" He pauses, unable to continue.

"I know, I know," I whisper, I can't say the word either. "Hudson, who was it?" I know that whoever it is, they're familiar to me but I just can't put my finger on who it was.

"I don't know, Princess. I'm going to find out." He sounds broken. "I can't trust anyone," he whispers, "I don't want to trust them."

"It wasn't Jagger. I promise you that." I can't have him thinking it was Jagger, he needs him now more than ever.

"How sure are you, Princess?" So much relief in those few words.

"I'm certain. Jagger has such a distinctive accent. The man didn't have an accent, Hudson."

"I'm going to find out who it is. They're not going to get away with this." The way he talks, the anger in his voice it reminds me of what my mom told me. This is who he is.

"What are you going to do to him?" I shouldn't have asked but I need to know.

He sighs. "Mia, this is who I am. I'm not going to change."

I blindly reach out for him, my hands grazing against his hard calloused hand. "I never asked you to. I just wanted to know what you were going to do when you find him."

He doesn't even hesitate in answering me. "I'm going to kill him. He's going to die the most painful death anyone can ever have and he's going to know that he doesn't touch what is mine."

"Just be careful," I beg, I'm so tired, and my body is sinking further into the bed. "Thank you."

"Princess, why are you thanking me?"

"For saving me." It comes out slurred but the way his hand tightens around mine tells me that he heard me.

"Always, Mia. I'll always save you." It's the last thing I hear before I fall back to sleep.

I wake to a dry mouth, I need some water. My right eye opens and I'm surprised, I didn't think I'd be able to open it. Hudson said they were swollen. Turning to look to my left, I see Hudson sitting on the chair, his eyes closed. His chest rising and falling slowly as he sleeps, I just watch him as he does, he looks so peaceful. I never got to see him this at ease before, I like it.

"I can feel you staring at me," he says as his lips lift at the side.

I blush, embarrassed that I've been caught staring at him. "You look so peaceful. You're always so serious, so tense. I haven't seen you look so peaceful."

His eyes open at my words. "I'm finally able to sleep. I hadn't slept in over three weeks." I know that he means he didn't sleep while I was taken. "You've opened your eye. How does it feel?"

I shrug. "It's not too bad. Why are you sleeping here? You should go home and get some rest."

He gives me a get real look. "Not going to happen. As soon as you're able, I'm bringing you home."

I smile. "I can't wait." Going home with him is all that I want. I've been so stupid. "I'm sorry."

He takes my hand and gives it a tight squeeze. "Why are you sorry?"

"I should have spoken to you. Instead I left, I let what my mom told me, get to me. I was so hurt, you never told me about that side to you. You made me fall in love with a person I didn't know. I felt betrayed, Hudson so I left. I shouldn't have. If I hadn't, Lacey would still be alive. That man wouldn't have done those awful things to me. I'm sorry," I whisper the last part, still not wanting to talk about what he did to me. I don't think I'll ever want to talk about it.

He shakes his head, his eyes narrowed. "No princess don't apologize. I never told you because I wanted you to get to know me. The real me, not the man who is the boss. I wanted you to know Hudson, not the Kingpin. I thought if you got to know me you would understand the other part of me. You would know that it's not all who I am."

He doesn't get it. "Don't you see, Hudson? With you not telling me, you hurt me more than if you had told me. I would have understood... maybe not understood, I would have been mad. But I wouldn't have walked away, I would have spoken to you, we would have talked it through until I understood a bit more about you. Instead my mom told me. Everything I believed to be true was dashed with just one sentence. You are a killer. You have killed people. That's what I couldn't wrap my head around. Someone who is so sweet to me, who cares so much about me, more than anyone has shown me in a very long time. You made me feel so special, so wanted, so loved. To think that man could be so cruel, to take someone's life? I just couldn't fathom it."

He was silent for a second, he rakes his eyes over my face, almost as if he's searching for answers. "What about now? Where does this leave us?"

He's worried that I'm ending things. That's not at all how this is going. "Being away from you, being held in that place." I shake my head, "Watching my best friend die, holding her in my arms she took her last breath, having that man do that to me." I swallow hard as tears form in my eyes. "It made me realize something, that no matter what, I love you."

"Fuck, Mia!" he gasps and kisses my hand. "I don't know what I did to deserve your love. I love you too and I'm never going to let you go."

I give him a smile. "You are all I thought about, you were my solace. You were my escape. Thinking about you, and the way you'd hold me whenever we were together. I'd remember the way you'd look at me as if I walked on water. The way your fingers would trail along my skin when we spoke. You were the reason I was sane. You found me, Hudson, you took me out of that nightmare." I will never be able to express my gratitude to him. He took me from the depths of hell.

"It wasn't quick enough, but I'll always find you, Baby. Always." He promises me.

"When can I go home?" I've been here long enough, I just want to go home. Although I don't think I have a home anymore. I don't know if I'll be able to go back there, back to the house where my dad was. Where I grew up, the only place that held special memories of my father. Right now it holds so many bad memories.

His eyes light up, those brown eyes of his so big. "The Doctor said that as soon as you're better you can come home. I'll talk to her again and see if we can get you home tonight you've been through enough I think coming home with me will be the best thing."

"How do you know that I was coming home with you?" I quip.

"No matter where you go, I'm coming with you. With the way things are right now. I'd prefer it if you would stay with me," he says softly. "I need to have you somewhere close. Somewhere I can keep an eye on you, not because I don't trust you but because I love you. I need to make sure you are safe and right now Mia I can't guarantee your safety. There is someone out there who wants to hurt me, and them doing so is to hurt you. I won't let that happen, not again. I'm going to kill them. I'm going to make them pay for everything they have done to you and to Lacey." His voice tight with anger, I believe every word he's saying. I know that he won't stop until he finds out who has done this.

"Hudson, wherever you go I'm coming with you. I can't be away from you anymore. I love you." It's that simple, yes he has done bad things. Hell, he'll probably keep doing them, but I love him and he loves me and that's all that matters to me. If there is some way that I can stop him from killing, I will. But I will not stop him from being the man he is, the man I love, the man that has shown me time and time again that he loves me too.

"God, it's so good to hear you say that. My ultimate goal is to keep you safe, and I may go about it a bit heavy, I may come across brash and angry, but Mia your safety is all that matters to me." He stands up, his hands cupping my face. His eyes locked on mine. "You have been hurt, God in ways that no man should ever hurt a woman. And knowing that it happened because of me. It fucking kills me to know that you have been through, to know what some bastard has put you through." He shakes his head, his eyes gleam with unshed tears, it hurts me seeing him like this. My brave, amazing man is hurting and there's nothing I can do to stop it because right now, I'm broken.

"Mia, I may not be the best man in the world. I have done heinous things and I can't say that I'll ever stop doing those things. There are a few things I can guarantee you, and that is my love, my honesty from now on, and my word. You have my word that I won't let anything harm you again. You have my word that I will love you until my dying breath, and you have my word that when I find this sonofabitch, I am going to make him pay for what he has done to you." So much determination behind those words. This is the rawest I've ever seen him and I like seeing this side to him.

"Hudson, has my Mom been by?" I don't think she has and it hurts. Why wouldn't she want to see me? "Does she know that I was taken? Does she know that Lacey died?" I ask him and the way he glances away answers my questions for me.

"Yes she knows," he tells me and his voice is tight, I know that I'm not going to like whatever the reason for her not being here is. "The reason she's not here is because I won't let her be." My eyes widen his words. Why, what has she done?

"You may think that I'm being a bastard by not letting her see you or vice versa, but Mia somebody betrayed me, us. Somebody knew where you were going that day. There was only one person who had any idea where you may have been going: your mother. She gave you the key to the house, she had to have known where you were going. So no, your mom doesn't get to see you."

My mouth opens in shock, it takes me a while to find my voice. "Hudson, you can't really believe that Mom had anything to do with this?"

He ignores my question and starts his tirade again. "Hell the bitch didn't even leave Hidden Hills until a few days ago. She knew you were missing and she didn't give a shit. So no she does not get to see you, she does not get to act as a grieving mother, and she doesn't get to act as if she gives a shit. When we all know that all she cares about is herself."

"Hudson," I whisper unsure what to say.

"I have been nice to that woman but all she does is look out for herself. I'm sorry Mia it stops now. That woman does not come here unless I say so. Unless you are one hundred percent sure that you are safe in her hands, if that is the case I will let her and I will be present when she's here. I don't trust her, I never will. Not with your life."

I'm in shock, I knew that he didn't like my mom I just never knew how much he hated her. "Hudson, I just want to go home," I tell him again. I'm not going to argue with him. I don't think my mom will hurt me, I don't think she'd betray him or me but I'm too tired to argue. Once I'm home, I'll talk to him about it.

ELEVEN

Hudson
———————

ONE WEEK LATER

TODAY'S the day that Mia comes home. I've been in many a situation where my life has been on the line, yet I'm a nervous wreck right now, my heart is racing. Today could be the day the rat comes out to play. What a better way to get to ambush us, especially when I'm bringing my precious cargo home. I have men ready and waiting, I have a route mapped out. Only three people know the exact route; Me, Jagger, and my dad. Mia has told me that Jagger is not the man and I believe her. I knew deep in my gut that it wasn't him, I didn't think he'd have it in him. He's my best friend, the man has always had my back. I know that I hurt him by questioning his loyalty, I was an ass, my head was gone when Mia was taken and I wasn't thinking clearly I know it and he knows it. I apologized and I gave him this mission, he knows that me giving him this means I trust him. Now all is well with us.

Along the route I have men on each and every rooftop, I have men in cars parked on the streets just in case the rat gets any ideas trying to ambush us on the way home. If he does he's fucked. I have no trust when it comes to my men so I did the only thing I could think of, I got other men in. John Healy's men to be precise. The man owes me a marker and I'm cashing in on it. It's fucking bad that I need to go elsewhere but deep within my organization. Someone close to me is betraying me and until I can prove who it is, I need to make sure that Mia is safe. So I've called in a marker. John Healey is the man that killed Kane for having sex with his sixteen year old daughter. He was one of our men, it meant we were meant to deal with it. We weren't given the opportunity. With me being the man I am, I understood where the Healy's were coming from. If I had a sister or a daughter who was sixteen and a thirty year old had sex with her, raped her basically I'd have killed him too. Fuck the consequences. So I did the only thing I could do. I made out of that I called the hit on Kane, that I had given the Healy's the go-ahead to kill him. In doing so I took the wrath of my father for it and I'd do it again because I know that if it was me I have done exactly the same thing. I would have reacted the exact same way. The Healy's don't know that, they think I did them a solid and now they're repaying the favor. They're going to help me keep Mia safe.

I have a fleet convoy. Three Healy's lead the way, followed by me with Mia, which is then tailed by my father, and then Jagger. A six car convoy leading us home not mentioning the cars that are located on the streets along the route, and the men on the rooftop. Anyone who comes for me is going to die, no ifs or buts. I don't believe the rat will show his face today, he's gotten so close to being found out that he needs to hide. He's doing what rats do scurrying away from danger

My dad walks out first, Mia directly behind him, her hand on his back. Jagger's behind Mia right on her back and my arms around her shoulders if anyone wants her to have to get through us. It's just a precaution, one that I will be doing any time me and Mia are in public. I just need to get someone to take over from my father because right at this moment two shots and you could take out both me and my dad, effectively killing off the generations of Brady's

The Healy's jump into their cars when we approach and start the engines. As soon as I open the passenger's door on the car dad and Jagger rush to theirs. Helping Mia into the passenger's side, I run around to the drivers and hop in. I know that having Mia in the front beside me is stupid but I'll be able to keep a better view of her here rather than in the backseat. We wait until Jagger gives us the go ahead that he is ready. When he's ready we'll set off, no matter if there's red lights, all the cars in this convoy go together not getting split up, no way, no how. I can imagine what people would say if they could see me, that Hudson Brady has gone soft. My name used to instil fear into people's hearts, just hearing my name would make their blood run cold. If they were to see me now, sitting behind the wheel of this Escalade, my hands shaking. I feel fear, I'm scared. I know that if it were just me, I would go guns blazing, I wouldn't give a shit. But this is Mia, I can't have anything hurt her. I'd lose my damn mind if she were to die.

"Hudson." Her soft voice calls out, it's not as scratchy as it had been when she woke up. "It's going to be okay."

I find it amusing that she is comforting me, it should be the other way around. Jesus fucking Christ, man the fuck up. Right now I need to be focused on keeping Mia safe and that means keeping my focus on this drive home. My house is safe for her to be in. It's harder to penetrate than Fort Knox. So she'll be safe as soon as we arrive at my house. There's only six blocks between here and there. That's all I have to worry about, making it through those six blocks. I know that the men helping me guard her are going to do the best they can to make sure she's not hurt in any way, shape, or form.

I reach over and take her hand. "I promised you, nothing was ever going to happen to you again."

"I know you won't. It's been a while since I was in your house." She gives me a cheeky smile

I smirk. "That's right. That night started my obsession for you."

Her laugh is like a little bell going off. "Obsession? Are you telling me that the bad Hudson Brady is obsessed with little old me?"

I love this side to her. Her fun, cheeky, light side. Her eyes don't hold the same mischief as her smile, instead her eyes hold a darkness, one that wasn't there until she was in that basement. I'm going to make it my mission to make sure she can move on from it, grow stronger from it, I will make sure it never happens again.

The honk signals that Jagger's ready, my dad revs his engine and I glance at Mia. "Put your seatbelt on," I tell her and I, too, rev my engine. We're ready.

The convoy begins to move my eyes peeled on the road glancing around making sure nobody suspicious is around. I'm acting like a paranoid jackass but I don't give a fuck. I'm talking everyone that is in the vicinity, I have surveillance covering this route as soon as the doctor gave the go ahead for Mia to come home it's been in the works.

Dad, Jagger and the Healy's have one together they made sure that if the rat comes out there's no way for him to hide. We're going to know who it is

My phone rings causing Mia to jump out of her seat, "Relax," I tell her and she gives me a quick short nod.

"Yeah?" I answer and can feel the glare that Mia's giving me.

"Hudson, its John. I'm two blocks from you." He's talking quick, he's on edge. "There's something here that don't seem right."

"What is it?"

"There's road works. There's no way there should be roadworks here. I've a feeling it's a set up."

My teeth clench, he's right. We made sure there wasn't going to be any. We would have gone a different route if we'd known. "If they know we're moving Mia, they're going to have this all planned out."

"What are you thinking?"

"We stay on course. If this were me, I'd have a road block set in place and have them abandon their plan, have them move somewhere else and then ambush. We know this route, we have men all over this place. Call your men and have them gather there, if they want to fight, we're doing it where we choose."

"Damn, you're your father's son. That's for fucking sure. I'll call my men. Look, Boy, no one is going to get your girl. We'll make sure of it," he says and I believe him.

"Good and, John, call me boy again, I'll take your fucking head off," I growl, I fucking hate being called boy. I end the call, not giving the fucker a chance to apologize. He's said it and I've corrected him, he says it again and I'll make him regret it.

I put Jagger and my dad in a conference call, they're

on speaker and Mia can hear everything. I know that she'll be scared but her hearing this conversation will mean that she'll know what to do if it is indeed someone trying to take me down. "There's a roadblock ahead. Roadworks apparently," I inform them and see Mia shifting in her seat. I rest my hand on her leg and she instantly calms.

"Okay, so do we go another route?" Jagger asks.

"No, if this asshole thinks like I do, they'll expect us to move to a different route. That's not happening. We have men along this route, enough to make sure whoever this fucker is he won't see it coming."

"He's right, we have enough men to outgun them. That is if this is a setup, if it is, I don't see the rat being here. I don't see him having the guts to be somewhere where he could easily be identified."

"We're going ahead with the plan. Jagger, if shit goes down, go for Mia. That is your only job, keep Mia safe. Get her to a safe place."

"Boss…" He's hesitant, this isn't what he signed up for. He was meant to make sure that nothing happens to me. That is no longer the case.

"Jagger, Mia is the most important thing to Hudson. So if bullets start flying, get Mia the hell away from there," Dad reiterates what I've said. It's good finally having him behind me.

"Fine," he grits out, I know he hates it, not only does he not like the thought of me being shot at, but also at the thought of missing out on the action.

"Okay, keep your eyes open. Make sure you have your weapons ready. If this goes down, there's no waiting." I end the call and reach for my gun. "Mia, you doing okay?" I ask softly.

"Not really, what if he's here, Hudson?" Her breathing starts to get shallow.

"Mia, look at me." I tell her, my voice calm, but forceful. She doesn't even hesitate, her head turns and I see the tears shining in her eyes, and I follow as one lone tear makes its way down her cheek and onto her chest. "If he's here, he's not going to get to you. I won't let him, Jagger is going to be your personal security detail."

She sucks in a deep breath. "I don't want you to get hurt."

I hide my smile, damn she's cute. "I'll be fine. Mia, if anything happens, I need you to do as I say, I need you to go with Jagger and do as he tells you."

She opens her mouth, no doubt to argue.

I snap, I'm doing this for her safety. "Look Mia, whoever is after me isn't going to care who gets caught in the crossfire. I need you to do as I ask and go with Jagger. If not, I'm going to be focused on you when I should be focused elsewhere."

Her eyes widen and I think I see a hint of guilt flash through them. "Of course, I'll do as you say. I'm hoping that it's just a roadblock and nothing else."

"We're almost there so we're about to find out."

"I love you, Hudson," she whispers as she leans across the center console and places a soft kiss against the corner of my mouth.

I turn my head and press a hard chaste kiss against her lips. "I love you too, Princess, nothing is going to harm you."

"I know." She doesn't sound as though she believes it. I guess after everything that fucker did to her tells her differently.

Tires squeal and my focus turns to the road. Shit, it's going down. Turning back to Mia, her eyes full of worry, she's wringing her hands together, and it's something I've noticed she does when she's nervous. "It's going to be okay, remember what I said?" I say to her, getting her attention. She nods. "Go to Jagger and do exactly as he says." I remind her, I know she doesn't want me to leave her, I can see she's toying with arguing with me but she decides against.

I watch as Healy's men exit their cars, their guns drawn and ready to fight. This is it, I finally get to see the bastard who betrayed me, the fucker who hurt the woman I love. "See you soon, Princess." I murmur as I exit the car and draw my gun.

"Son, Jagger's got Mia, they'll be leaving soon. We're good to go." His tone has an edge of excitement to it. It's been a while since he's had any action

Gun shots ring out from at least three different locations. "You've got some fucking balls to be taking us on here," I shout, the Healy men smiling at my words.

John Healey walks towards me a big smile on his face, he too has his gun drawn. "Fucking assholes must have balls. Now, it's time to show them whose boss. You don't fucking mess with us, and you certainly don't take our women."

Shots ring out and once again, it's more than one gunman, I crouch down behind the car just as the glint of the gun catches my eye. "On the rooftop." I yell informing the Healy's, and as one they all look up.

"We're surrounded," John growls. "They must have known our route, how the fuck did they find out?" He glances around at his men, each one of them have their guns aimed for the rooftops.

"Now isn't the time," Dad says quietly. "Once we get out of here, we'll find out how he's finding out this information."

"Fuck." John shakes his head as he grabs his phone

and calls someone. "We're surrounded, get here and fucking take out every bastard on the rooftops."

I wonder who he's talking to, I don't have time to contemplate it as a bullet whizzes past my head and sinks into the side of the car. "We need to get to those fucking rooftops," I tell them, there's no way we can shoot them down. None of us have a rifle.

John smiles "Listen boys." I bite my tongue and do as he says, the whoomping of a helicopter sounds from above us and we all glance up and see the chopper circling above us. "Those assholes aren't going to be up there any longer. I've got snipers on board."

I smirk, they'll be scrambling to get off the rooftops, they're sitting ducks up there. "Surround those buildings," I yell as I get to my feet. "Those fuckers are going to come down, I don't want any of them escaping." All the men nod, taking a step closer toward the buildings.

The helicopter gets louder as it draws nearer. The sound drowning out the gunshots. Glancing around, I see three men on the ground, dead and there's a couple injured that are taking cover behind the escalade. It doesn't take long before the helicopter hovers overhead, glancing up, I see that John was right, there's two men standing on the bars of the chopper, rifles in hand as they aim for the rooftops. The shots have stopped, making me wary. What is their plan now?

John's cell rings, "Yeah?" he answers it immediately. A sinister smile forms on his lips as his eyes light up. "We've got it from here boys." He hangs up, "They're scurrying down the stairs. Three of them, coming from two buildings."

Just as I had suspected. "Let's greet them then shall we?" This is what I love, the thrill I get from the action. We split up,

John taking half his men and going to the next building as Dad and I with the rest of Healy's men take the building in front of us. "I want them alive. I have a feeling that the rat isn't here and he's sent other's to do his bidding. I need answers and that means having them tell me who hired them." There's a bite to my tone, I don't give a shit if they want them dead. I'm in charge here and that means what I say goes.

Opening the door to the building, we're greeted by the sound of footsteps and panting. By the way the footsteps are pounding against the steps they're running for their lives. It's not long before they come into view, more than fifteen guns pointed at them. It doesn't take them a second to drop their guns and hold up their hands in surrender.

Too easy floats throw my mind.

Glancing at dad needing to see if he too thinks this was way too easy. "It's time for us to leave, we need to find Jagger and Mia."

Dad's eyes widen as he too comes to the same conclusion as I have.

Turning on my foot, I walk out of that damn building and onto the street. Chaos, that's all I see. Abandoned cars everywhere, people fled when the shots were fired. Pulling out my cell from my pocket I dial Jagger's phone. It rings out. Shit.

"Dad," I yell, he's instructing the Healy's where to bring the shooters so that we can deal with them later. "It's time to go." I jump into the car that I was in with Mia and see my dad sprinting across the street to catch up. Starting the engine, I hit re-dial, once again I'm left listening to the damn ringing.

"Hudson, we need backup." Jagger says finally answering, "We've got four cars on us."

Red hot rage blinds me. I was fucking stupid, I should

have kept Mia here with me, she would have been safer. "Mia?" I breathe.

"I'm okay," she reassures me, sounding as though she's in shock.

"We're on our way." I end the call and press my foot down on the gas. They're not taking her, not again.

TWELVE

Mia

GLANCING in the side mirror I see the cars behind us. As soon as Jagger pulled me into his Escalade and raced out of there we had a convoy following us. They haven't even tried to hide the fact they're chasing us. Fear grips me as one of the cars behind moves up so we're side to side.

"Mia it's going to be okay." His voice is tight but full of confidence.

"I really wish everyone would stop saying that." I sigh, we have no idea who is behind this all. At the moment we're being chased by a ghost.

Jagged glances at me before he returns his focus to the road. "Mia, I'll lay down my life for you. If they want you, they're going to have to go through me first."

"You can't mean that!" I gasp horrified at the mere thought.

His lips curl up at the corners. "I'd do the exact same for Hudson."

I shake my head in disbelief. I understand him wanting to do it for Hudson but not why he'd risk his life for me? "Why? You barely know me."

"Mia, you are Hudson's which means you are family. I protect my family at all costs." He turns to look at me, but keeps glancing back to the road. "I know what you did for Sarah and Alllie, all the money you sent, and when you'd visit you'd stock up her pantry and cupboards with food that wasn't perishable. Not only that, you've been her constant support throughout everything. What you've done for my daughter… for my woman." He shakes his head, as he chokes up. "That means more than anything and for that I'd die for you."

My eyes well with tears, he's so sweet. I know that what happened between him and Sarah wasn't entirely his fault. I mean the man was kissing someone hours after Sarah left his bed but the other stuff that was Carina's fault. "Sarah's one of my best friends." My breath hitches at the words. God, Lacey. I still haven't come to terms with her death, I do everything in my power to bury those memories deep down. It doesn't work though. Every time I close my eyes, all I hear is those gunshots, the gurgling sound she made as she took her last breath. I honestly believe that her death is going to haunt me forever and I hope it does, it'll be a reminder of how evil this life is, how one moment can change your life.

"Mia…" he says softly, his southern drawl so thick.

"I'm okay." I lie, it's better than the alternative, breaking down and crying. I've shed enough tears over a monster, he doesn't deserve anymore.

"You're not, but you will be." He winks at me, how is it that he's so calm? We're in the middle of a car chase and he's acting as if we're going on a leisurely road trip. "Do you blame Hudson for what happened to you and Lacey?"

I gasp, the thought had never crossed my mind. I don't blame him and I never would, he is not responsible for what happened. Just as I'm about to answer him, the car beside us tries to cut us off, thankfully Jagger is quick on the brake and maneuvers us into the next lane.

"Hang tight, Mia, things are about to get fun." The smile on his face can only be described as mischievous.

My heart is in my throat right now as the car speeds up, "Jagger, what are you going to do?" My eyes are glued to the car on my right, what the hell is he planning to do?

"Down, Mia." Jagger yells, his hand going to the back of my head. He jars my head forward and I keep it there.

Squeezing my eyes closed, I hug my legs, fear coursing through my veins. "Jagger?" My entire body shaking, I have no idea what's going on.

Glass smashes and I squeal as it rains down around me. "Mia, it's okay," he tells me, his voice tight and I'm seriously beginning to hate those two words. It's all everyone ever says and yet, they're not true. Nothing is okay, nothing about this situation is okay.

"What the hell happened?" I ask, my voice calm while inside I'm screaming.

"They shot the windows in, keep your head down. The cavalry is coming."

Hope blooms inside. "They're here?"

"Yes, they're behind us, they've taken out two of the six cars and are working their way up to us. This will all be over soon." He promises me and again, another lie.

"We have no idea who's doing this Jag, so no it won't be over soon." I can't keep the anger and pain out of my voice. I'm not going to be safe, Hudson's not going to be safe until we figure out who this monster is. Once we do, we can finally start trying to move on, if that's even a possibility.

"That's not for you to worry about," he says through clenched teeth and I bite back my response.

He isn't the person I should be having this conversation

with, Hudson is and he's in for a shock if he thinks I'll be left out of knowing everything that's going on. This isn't just affecting him, this has affected me in ways that I may never recover from.

My body jolts as the car swerves. Lifting my head, my mouth parts slightly as I get a look at the man in the car beside us. That birthmark on his neck, it's so prominent, like its taunting me. "Jagger," I whisper, as my fear creeps up through my throat. Tears well in my eyes as I stare at the man in the car. "He was the man that kept us in that basement. He works for the man that killed Lacey." For the man that raped me. It's what's running through my mind, if he's here that means so is the man that did those things.

Jagger's head turns to me, I watch as his eyes narrow as he takes me in before turning back to face the man that helped keep me a prisoner. "We'll make sure that he doesn't get away." It's a rumble, I've never heard him so angry before. "Do you have your seatbelt on?"

That's something he should have asked me earlier. I always have my seatbelt on. I glare at him, "Of course, what are you going to do?"

He doesn't answer me. His knuckles turn white as his grip on the steering wheel tightens, once again the car starts to speed up, glancing at the speedometer on the dash, I watch as the pointer rises, we're almost at 120 and it's rising still. Dread sets in the pit of my stomach as Jagger jaw clenches, his jawline become more pronounced as he does. His eyes narrowing as he focuses on the road, it's a look of a man that's got a plan, and I'm not sure I'm going to like it. The accomplice doesn't take long to be side by side with us again, a sinister smile forms on Jagger's face and that just makes me want to cry. I hate not knowing what's going to happen.

Jagger twists the steering wheel to the right, my body is thrown forward as we collide with the car beside us. My head connects with the dash in front of me and I cry out in pain. The car swerves once again, this time to right itself before Jagger slams on the brakes. The tires squeal under the pressure as the car careens forward before coming to a stop. Jag doesn't hesitate, he's out of the car, his gun in hand as he moves towards the other car. I'm sitting here, disconnected from everything around me, just watching Jagger. I don't feel anything, the pain, the fear, the dread are all gone and I'm numb.

The door opens, but I don't turn to see who's there, my gaze is still focused on Jagger as he drags the man out of the car.

"Mia." That deep gravelly voice penetrates through my haze, "Princess?"

"It's him." I whisper as the man stands, the sun shining down on him, highlighting his every feature. Each feature that I memorized every day, every night as he bought us bread and water.

"Who, Princess?"

"He's the man that would feed us while in the basement." I'm fixated on him, relief washing through me as Jagger guides him away towards a waiting vehicle. They have him, which means that they'll be able to find out who is behind all of this.

Hudson's breath is hot against my face as he reaches for my seatbelt. "Princess, we're going home and we're going to talk," he tells me, his voice soft but there's an edge of something to it, but I can't figure out what it is.

He lifts me out of the car and I put my hands around his neck, wanting to be as close to him as humanly possible. He doesn't frighten me, it's the exact opposite, touching him is like my safety blanket. "Did he hurt you?"

I shake my head. "I don't think so." It sounds so stupid not knowing, but I don't. He could have been the man that knocked me unconscious at my parents house.

He pulls me closer to him, kissing the top of my head as he walks us to the car. Not once saying a word but yet his actions speak volumes. He's once again showing me the love that he's always shown me, I press a soft kiss against his neck.

"Dad, let's get the hell out of here before the cops show up," Hudson tells Harrison as he places me on my feet and helps me into the car.

"You okay, Mia?" Harrison asks as I settle into my seat. "You look a hell of a lot better than the last time I saw you."

Frowning as I glance at Hudson in confusion, when did he see me last?

"Dad found us the doctor and the house so that you wouldn't have to go to a hospital." He explains as he reaches for me, lifting me once again out of my seat and onto his lap. "You look tired." He comments as he places a kiss against my lips.

"I am, I want to sleep." But I'm too afraid of what nightmares may come.

"Sleep princess, I'll keep you safe." He promises me, pulling me close to his body.

Tucking my head into the crook of his neck, I close my eyes and pray that if I manage to sleep, that it'll come peacefully.

I come awake and confusion sets in. I'm shrouded in darkness, fear grips me with a choke hold. I'm back in that damn basement, a whimpering sound breaks through the silence. It sounds as though there's a cat's dying.

"Princess." A guttural sound. A voice that I know, a voice I trust. It's then that I realize it's me that was whimpering. "Princess, it's okay." There's that word again.

"Light. I need light." I breathe, trying to fight back the anxiety and fear I have.

The room instantly becomes illuminated. It takes me a while to gain my bearings. This room is familiar, it takes me a while before I realize why. I'm in Hudson's bedroom, a room I haven't been in since the night we met in Synergy. It hasn't changed a bit. Arms tighten around me and I lean into them. Hudson's holding me as we lay on the bed.

"I'm sorry," I whisper, I feel weak, useless, and pathetic. What twenty year old is afraid of the dark?

His hands tighten on me, turning me around to look at him. "Don't. Never apologize for anything. Not with me, not ever."

"I feel stupid, I'm afraid of waking up in a dark room."

He places a kiss against my lips, shivering at the coldness of his touch. "Talk to me, tell me what happened." His fingers caress my arm, I let myself give into the hypnotic feeling. "Nothing is going to hurt you, Princess. I promise you, I'll die before I let anything happen to you."

"You're the second person to tell me that today." I remark and watch as Hudson smirks. "You've spoken to Jagger?" I should have guessed, but when did they have time to talk?

"I did, talk to me Mia. What happened to you?"

I lie into his body, not wanting to see the pity in his eyes as I tell him everything. As soon as I get comfortable, his arm goes around my back and he holds onto my ass, his thumb rubbing circles as I begin to talk.

"I got to my parents house, I remember finding it odd that there was another vehicle parked out front. I was so unaware of what was about to happen. I was hurt and betrayed, I wasn't thinking straight. I remember walking up to the house and wondering why Lacey hadn't come out to greet me, she always did, and we always did. It was our thing. I didn't think much of it, when I pushed the door open, I was hit across the face and everything went blank." I close my eyes, reliving the pain again. How it burst through my face and pulled me into a black abyss.

"Fuck," he says through gritted teeth. "What happened next?"

"I woke up in a dark room. Only a tiny sliver of light was shining into the room, I glanced over at Lacey and saw that she too was hurt, worse than I ever was. She couldn't breathe properly, she kept coughing. I knew that it wasn't a good sound but we were both shackled, I couldn't get to her. I couldn't move and when I tried I was in so much pain that I wanted to cry out." Telling Hudson this, it should make me feel vulnerable, but it doesn't.

"The man that was in the car, he spoke to us for days, weeks. I don't know, I couldn't work out how much time had passed. He'd bring Lacey and I bread and water twice a day." I don't tell him about how he'd leave each of us a bucket for us to go to the toilet. It was humiliating and degrading, something that I don't ever want to admit too. "I saw his face daily, I remembered each and every single detail that he has. From the birth mark on his neck, the freckle on his earlobe, to the scar on his eyebrow. Every single marking I have etched into my brain."

"That's good baby, you did good." He's full of praise but I don't feel as though he should be happy about it.

"Then the man came, I never saw his face, he always came in the dead of night. There was no light shining through. When he grabbed me, and began undressing me, I fought, I tried with all my heart." I want him to understand that I never wanted this to happen.

"God, Mia." He's in pain, I hate that he's hurting.

"I didn't want it. I tried to stop it." I promise him, hoping that he believes me.

His arms tighten around me, "Fuck, Princess, you're killing me here. I know that you didn't want it. I'm going to kill him, he's going to wish he never met me, or you by the time I'm finished." He vows, the anger in his voice is palpable.

God, I love him so much. "When he was doing what he did, I closed my eyes and thought of you. You're the reason I was able to get through it. Your love, it was my beacon. I wouldn't have survived if it hadn't been for you." Tears quietly fall as I hold onto him for dear life. "I'm not sure how much time had passed before he came back again. I fully expected him to do it again. I braced myself for it to happen, my mind switching off and going to my happy place, to you. But when he said that things had changed then I realized he was panicked. He shot Lacey. God, that noise, it was so loud."

"I'm so sorry, Baby."

"He threw a key down onto the floor so that I could unlock my shackle and flee. I couldn't see where he had thrown it and Lacey had been shot, I was in shock, all I wanted to do was find it. My heart sunk when he shot her again, I knew by the sounds she was making that she was going to die. I tried so hard to find it. By the time I did, he was gone and Lacey was bad." I sob, I can't continue, the image of Lacey in my arms is etched in my brain. I can't switch it off.

He buries his head into my shoulder and kisses me. "I love you, Princess, I'm in awe of you."

"I let her die." I cry into him.

He pulls me up, so that I'm lying on top of him. "No, you didn't. Your best friend died in the arms of someone she loved. You didn't let her die, you were there when she needed you the most."

"But if it weren't for me, then she'd still be alive," I whisper, the tears cascade down my face, I watch them land on Hudson's cheek.

"If it's anyone's fault it's mine. Mia, I'm the reason that you and Lacey were put in that situation in the first place." His face is blank of any emotion.

"How can you say that? Why would you say that? You aren't the reason. You didn't pull the trigger that killed her, you didn't tell that man to…" I catch myself before I say that word, "do those things to me."

His eyes fill with disgust. "Of course not."

"There's your answer, you're not responsible for this." I shake my head, how can he think that?

"What if I were in the room with her and I couldn't get to her until it was too late, would I have let her die?"

Frowning, I wonder what he's trying to say? "No."

He gives me a pointed look. "So why do you?"

I close my eyes, I understand what he's saying but my heart sees differently. I yawn and cuddle up to Hudson again. "I'm so tired."

He pulls me closer to him, shifting slightly so that he can cover us with the sheet. "Sleep, Princess, I've got you."

THIRTEEN

Hudson

WALKING into the kitchen I'm greeted by the sight of my father and Tina sitting at the bar having breakfast. I caved and let them stay wanting to keep my dad close by as I know whoever this fucker is he's going to go after my family. It means having Tina here. I dislike the woman but I'm going to keep my mouth shut for now, as it means keeping them safe. She's been warned that if she says anything to piss me or Mia off then she's likely to get a bullet in her head. I will not have her upsetting Mia, my girl has been through enough.

I never thought I would be reduced to tears by a woman and yet listening to Mia relive what she went through had my eyes welling up. When she whispered that she didn't want the bastard to rape her as if I believed otherwise, it gutted me. I meant what I said, she's fucking strong and I'm in awe of her. Who gives a shit if she doesn't like having the lights off? I'll keep them on just to make sure that she's safe. That whimpering sound she made last night shit the fucking life out me, I thought somebody was hurting her.

"How is Mia, son?" Dad asks as soon as he sees me. Glancing at Tina I see that she's got a fucking stupid grin on her face, one that I'd just love to wipe off

"She's in the shower right now. She had a bad night but she managed to get some sleep." She didn't move after she fell asleep on me. She kept her head tucked into my shoulder and slept peacefully. I don't know what I did to deserve her complete and utter trust, especially after I lied to her, but knowing that I'm someone she is safe around makes me feel like one lucky man.

"Do you think I'll be able to talk to my daughter today?" The disrespectful tone coming from Tina has me advancing on her in just two steps. My hand going around her neck lifting her from her seat, the thumping of her erratic heartbeat under my palm tells me that she's scared of what I'm going to do to her. She should have thought about that before running her mouth.

"Son?" Dad questions but when I glare at him, I see that he's got a smile on his face. Seems I'm not the only one that's got a dislike for Tina at the moment, things with her and dad are shaky at best.

"Dad, I told her before she came here. There were certain conditions she agreed to before walking through that door, if she doesn't like it, she can walk back out of it. How dare she come into my house and disrespect me?" I'm being good, my hands haven't tightened around her neck although I'd love nothing more than just snap it.

"Hudson." My hands release Tina at the soft willowy voice of Mia. "She's not worth getting upset over, this is mom just being frightened, and she doesn't mean to disrespect you." Her fingers tentatively graze against mine. I grab her hand as if it's a lifeline and calm the fuck down. "Mom," Mia says glaring at her.

Tina raises her hands in surrender. "I'm sorry." She doesn't fucking sound it.

"Whatever, I've got a meeting. Dad, are you ready?" I'm going to find out what that asshole, that kept Mia prisoner, has to say. There's only two things I need to know and I'll be getting answers from him or he's a dead man. Then again, depending what he says that could be the ending anyway.

"Yes, Son," he replies bringing his cup to his lips and taking a sip of his drink.

"I'm coming." There's steel in her voice and I look down at Mia, her face is blank and she squeezes my hand.

"Mia…" I begin, but she cuts me off.

"No, I'm coming. I want to be there. This isn't just about you, Hudson, this is about all of us. He held me captive for someone and I want to find out who, just as much, if not more, than you do." Her big green eyes plead with me. "Please, I need to find out who did this to me. I don't want to be afraid anymore." She confesses softly.

I know that I should be arguing with her, telling her that she can't come, she can't see this evilness that I have inside of me but I can't. Mia's been through hell and if she needs this then so be it. Anyone has a problem with it, that's their damn fucking problem, if they voice their opinion then there'll be hell to pay. "Please, Hudson," she begs again.

"Are you sure?" I ask her not wanting this to make things worse, this could tip her over the edge.

She looks me dead in the eyes, so much steel and determination in them. "This is what I want… What I need."

I nod, as I place a kiss against her soft lips. "If you're sure."

She doesn't even hesitate. "Completely."

"Everything is going to be okay." I reassure her, he's not going to hurt her, he'll never get a chance.

She groans and rolls her eyes. "Can we make a pact?"

I frown, confused at what she wants. "What sort of pact?"

She stands a little taller. "A pact where you don't tell me everything is going to be fine, or everything is going to be okay when you cannot guarantee it. I'm sick of those words, Hudson, it's all everyone's been saying to me since I've come home. I hate those words; 'Everything is going to be okay, don't worry you're safe.' Those words don't mean anything until we find the person who's responsible for all of this and until we do, you cannot guarantee my safety. You cannot guarantee that I'm going to be okay, because the truth is, until that man is found I'm not okay and I can't move on. All I think about is when is he going to get me again." Tears well in her eyes, but she doesn't let them fall. Instead she's holding her head up high and staring me down as if I'm her opponent.

Glancing at my father, I see the look on his face. He's proud of her just as I am. We've both witnessed some of the worst things in this world, hell we've committed those acts, and we've seen how some react to those things. Most would crumble to the floor, not want to know anything that's happening, just wanting to hide away from the world. Not Mia though, she takes the bull by the horns, she's not letting anyone beat her down.

I have the utmost respect for the woman I love, how she can speak to me without fear. I'll always listen to what she has to say. "Okay Mia I won't say it again, until I know for sure."

Relief hits her eyes and she gives me the biggest smile I've ever seen. "Thank you." She reaches up on her tiptoes and press the kiss against my lips. I can't help but deepen it when I feel the softness and plumpness of her lips. I've missed her so much, my hands snake around her waist and I put her towards me. Loving the little whimpers she makes as she her body hits against mine. She's wearing a dress, my hand grazes the hem of it. Loving how I can caress her skin, how she shivers as my fingers touch her leg.

Someone coughing has Mia pulling away from me, looking sheepish at being caught making out. Almost as if she forgot we were in a room with other people. I glare at my father, he's got a smirk on his face. "Now if you two love birds are finished, how about we find out what this fucker knows? Hmm? Then you two can get back to…" He waves his hand in our direction, "That."

I shake my head, he's an asshole. He's changed a lot since Mia was taken. I'm not complaining, I'm just wondering how long it's going to last. Turning my attention back to the woman in my arms. "This isn't finished." My lips graze the outer shell of her ear about here as I whisper to her. A shiver runs through her body and I smile, she's still affected by me I don't think that is ever going to change.

Her lips part in shock, I watch as her eyes fill with mischievousness. "Don't make promises you can't keep." She laughs and she dances away from me. That sound is fucking amazing.

"Mia, when you get back, you need to call Lacey's mom. She's been waiting for you so that she can have Lacey's funeral," Tina says softly and just like that, the happiness flees her body, the light disappears from her eyes.

"It's time to go," Dad growls, his eyes on Tina, I'll be surprised if their marriage lasts much longer.

"Mia, you can call from the car." I tell her, she nods but glances at the floor, she's not looking at anyone. "Dad,

Jagger's waiting outside for us. Will you walk Mia to the car, I just need to get something real quick. I'll be out in a minute." It's more so for Mia's benefit than my father's, I want her to know that I'll be right behind her.

"Of course," Dad says, placing his hand at Mia's back but she quickly withdraws from him. Dad doesn't miss a beat keeps behind her and lets her walk ahead making sure that she's okay.

As soon as the door closed behind them I speak, all the anger that I've had building up over the past few weeks boils out of me. "Get the fuck out of my house," I tell her, anger pouring out of me

"What? Why? What did I do? You can't kick me out, my daughter needs me, and my husband needs me." She cries, she's backtracking quickly, her eyes wide with fear and her face is pale as a ghost.

It's too late, she was warned and she didn't heed my words before, but she will now. "What did you do? Your daughter was finally…" I spit, pissed off that she has the power to make Mia so upset, "…Finally smiling and you told her that she needs to call her best friends parents. Giving her a reminder of the pain she's trying her best to bury, she held her best friend and she died. Do you know what it feels like to hold someone you love and watch them die in your arms?" It's a rhetorical question, I couldn't give a fuck if she has. "You do not give a shit about anyone but yourself. Your daughter does not need you, my father does not need you. You need us, because you have nowhere else to go. Now, Tina, mark my words, one more word from you and I will kill you." I turn away from her leaving her spluttering and walk to the front door. I don't turn back to look at her, as far as I'm concerned she's done.

Sliding into the backseat beside Mia, I see she's on the phone, she's staring out the window. I watch as a lone tear slowly makes its way down her face, I don't move, I let her be. Right now she needs to talk to Lacey's parents, I'm hoping that doing so will help her heal a little, or at least get that stupid notion that she let her die out of her head.

I look ahead and see both Jagger and dad talking in hushed tones. Jagger turns to face me. "We have a problem."

I groan, when don't we? "What?"

"The three people on the rooftops yesterday, they belong to a group of mercenaries," he informs me.

"They're muscle for hire?"

Dad nods. "They're tight lipped, they've not said a word and I doubt they will."

"Probably, but it'll be fun trying to get them to." I smirk. "Jagger, you up for getting a little creative?"

He starts the engine and grins. "Hell fucking yes."

I nod and wait for Mia to get off the phone, I can only hear one side of the conversation and so far all it's been is Mia apologizing.

"Will it be okay if I were to come to her funeral?" Mia asks and everyone in the car freezes, the fact she even has to ask that damn question pisses me off, what the hell have Lacey's parent's been saying to her? When Mia begins to weep softly, I want to find them and kill them. "Thank you," she whispers and ends the call.

I reach for her, pulling her onto my lap and she curls up into my body. "What did they say?"

"They thanked me." She hiccups as she tries to regain her composure. "Thanked me for being there with her, they wanted me to know that they're grateful that Lacey had me there with her until the very end. They also wanted me to thank you."

"Me?" I frown, what the hell did I do?

Mia nods against my chest. "Yes, they wanted to thank

you for finding us and allowing them to be able to bury their daughter."

Fuck. I swallow harshly, trying to get past the lump in my throat. "Why did you ask if you'd be allowed to go to the funeral?"

She shrugs. "I thought they'd hate me, they'd blame me for her death. I didn't think they'd want me there."

I pull her tighter against me. "But they do."

She nods. "Yes, they don't blame me at all."

"Princess, no one blames you except you. You aren't the reason she's dead." It doesn't matter how many times I tell her she won't believe it until she's ready too. "Are you sure you're ready for this?"

"I need to do this, whether I'm ready for it or not." There's that steel again, she's a fucking fighter.

The car ride was quiet, no one really spoke. Mia stays curled up in my arms, but as soon as we pull up into the driveway of the abandoned bar her entire body tenses beneath my hands. I bought this bar years ago it was originally planned to be synergy, but there was so much wrong with it that I couldn't go ahead and build what I wanted to build for my nightclub. So I bought in a different neighbourhood, this building however has been kept in a state of despair on the outside.

Once you're inside it's completely gutted except for the cellar, that cellar cost me hundreds of thousands of dollars to ensure it's soundproofed. It's deep underground, the perfect place to hurt someone, nobody is ever going to hear them scream. Everyone that was captured yesterday is here, there is no way for them to escape. They're tied to chairs with zip ties and I have the best locks in place even a fucking escape artist couldn't escape from here. It's locked up tighter than Fort Knox.

"Mia, are you ready?"

She nods and climbs off my lap and out of the car "Ready or not here we go," she grumbles and Jagger laughs, he thinks she's hilarious. He really does love her and I know that he's the one that told her that he'd take a bullet for her and I'm glad that he views her that way. Grateful that she's able to have someone else in this world other than me.

I grab her hand after exiting the car and together we walk towards the vacated bar. "Whatever's about to go down here you cannot stop it. You are going to see me as the boss, therefore you have to treat me as such. You cannot publicly disobey me or challenge me, to do so is seen as an act of disrespect. Do you understand?" I try to keep my voice as soft as I can but also let her know what she has to do to be a part of this world.

"Hudson, I would never disrespect you, that's just not me. If I have a problem with something, I wouldn't say it publicly. I'd wait until we were alone to talk to you about it," she replies instantly.

"Good, but what I do is my choice as the boss, you may not like that and that's fine. You can vent to me about it but you will not change the way I am."

She tuts. "I don't want to change who you are, Hudson. I fell in love with you. That includes the parts of you that are sweet, loving, and caring, but also the parts of you that aren't. I fell in love with the *Boss* and I understand these things. I've had so much time to think about this. You are what I want and that means taking you as you are. Just as you're taking me as I am." Fuck she's amazing.

"How the fuck do you get to be so wise?" Dad asks, eavesdropping on our conversation.

Heat rises up her cheeks and she glances away down at floor. "I didn't realize everyone was listening," she confesses quietly.

"Ignore them. Both Dad and Jagger love you, they're teasing you because they do care about you," I inform her and am rewarded with a bright smile.

"He's right, just as Jagger and Hudson have said they would lay their lives down for you, I will too. Mia, you have made my son the happiest I have ever seen him. Not only that, but hearing you tell him that you are not going to change him just proves what a truly special young lady you really are. I'm going to protect you, Mia, not because you are my wife's daughter or my son's future wife, but because of the special unique young lady you truly are." Damn Dad. That's the most meaningful thing I've ever heard him say to anyone.

Mia's eyes fill with tears. I smile, she cries when people are nice to her but steels herself when they're not. She's one of a kind, that's for sure.

FOURTEEN

Mia

THIS BAR HUDSON brought me to, it looks like it should be condemned. Looking up, I see there are slates missing, the windows are boarded up, and the walls look black with dirt. I'm scared to enter it in case it falls all around me, trapping us inside and killing us all in the process, but I know that Hudson wouldn't bring me anywhere that's unsafe. Hearing Harrison tell me that this is the happiest he's ever seen Hudson and it's because of me, meant everything. I was gobsmacked when he told me that he'd protect me not because of the people he loves love me, but because of me. I've never felt as much love as I have since I met Hudson, his family and friends have done nothing but show me love and respect.

As soon as I walk into the bar I know we're not alone, groaning from the left makes me turn to see what is making the noise. My eyes widen as I see three people tied to chairs, I'm horrified as I watch as blood trickles down one of the men's faces. He's got a cut to his eyebrow, a part of me wants to rush over and stop the bleeding but I know that I can't, it'll go against what

Hudson just told me. He is the boss and he obviously wants whatever is happening to happen. So I fight the urge and keep my head held high. Never show fear. It's something my dad used to tell me and it's something that has kind of come to the forefront of my brain in the past couple of days.

Glancing around this bar, I notice it's completely empty. There's no tables or chairs, no fixtures or fittings at all, hell there's a concrete floor beneath my feet. It's a shell, so much could be done with this place, so much potential. I'm curious as to why Hudson has it empty.

Hudson doesn't say a word to the men that are tied up, he walks past them and towards the door that I presume leads to the back. I didn't see the man that kept me prisoner tied to the chair, so I'm guessing he's in a room behind the door that Hudson's leading us through. When he pushes the door open, I hold my breath, ready to come face to face with the man that was part of the reason why Lacey died. I'm standing behind Hudson, his body keeping mine hidden as I walk in behind him.

This cellar is in complete darkness except for a tiny light above the man that's sitting there. He's not bleeding like I thought he would be, especially after seeing the man on the way in. He doesn't look in pain, and a part of me is disappointed at seeing him sitting there with a smug smile on his face. I'm grateful that he can't see me. I observe him, the cockiness he's got. It doesn't make sense, he should be scared, he could die and yet he doesn't look like a man on the edge of life.

"You made it through the night," Hudson's voice is deep, anger pouring out with every word he says. I've never heard him like this before and I automatically take a step back.

"Mia, it's still him," Jagger whispers, as his hands grab

my shoulders effectively stopping me from taking another step backward.

I watch as Hudson's body tenses, his head turning and he pins me with a dark look. He's angry, and I bite my lip hating that I'm the reason that he's mad. "You haven't told us who hired you yet. That is going to change." Hudson's tone sends shivers through my spine, I understand now what the difference is between the boss and my Hudson. They're so opposite, right now, I don't see the Hudson I know and love.

The man spits at Hudson and it misses barely, just landing inches from his polished shoes. "Go to hell."

"Been there. You took what is mine," Hudson growls, as he takes a step closer to him. "You are the reason that an innocent woman died."

A knock at the door, makes me jump, I didn't think anyone else was coming here. Jagger releases me and goes to find out who's at the door. Hudson walks over to me. "Mia?" he questions, his eyes darker than I'd ever witnessed.

I can't lie to him, there's no way I'd do that to him. I love him too much to do it. "I didn't expect you to be so different. Your voice was hard and it scared me."

He shows no emotion at my words. "You can leave if you wish." His voice tight, it's the boss that's talking to me now, not Hudson.

I stare at him, looking deep into those gorgeous brown eyes of his. "I'm not going anywhere."

"Mia, things have just started, they're going to get a hell of a lot worse. If you can't deal with how I am now, you won't be able to cope with what's yet to come."

"I know that, I'm prepared for that."

A dark laugh escapes him. "Oh Mia, you think you are but you're not. What's about to come is going to scare the hell out of you. You are about to witness me and Jagger at our worst."

Those words make me shiver and he doesn't miss it at all, I'm loving this dark side of him. "Bring it on." I think he's testing me, seeing if I'm able to be by his side through it all.

He smirks and I know that he's going to push me to my limits but I won't break. "Okay, Princess, let's see."

I raise my brow at him, I'm not going to fall, I've been through hell and I'm slowly starting to crawl my way back. I lower my voice so that no one can overhear what I'm about to say, I move forward so that we're only inches apart. "You haven't heard what I've said. You are it for me Hudson, you are my safe place. No matter if you're Hudson or the boss. I'm taking you every way I can."

His hand reaches up, cupping my chin. "You're a mystery aren't you?"

I shake my head, "No. I'm not. I love you Hudson."

His eyes fill with lust. "Love you too, Princess, but you don't have to prove anything to me, to anyone."

I kiss his lips, even as the boss he's putting me first. "I'm not, I'm here because I need to be here for me. Having you here with me means that I'm stronger but I'm not proving anything. Now go find out who hired him."

His lips twist. "Yes Ma'am." He winks at me before he turns back to face the asshole. His eyes darken with rage yet again. "Do you know who I am?"

The laughter from Hudson's captive chills my bones. "No, but you don't know who I am either."

The door opens and I turn to see the outline of Jagger walking in, he's not alone, I can see four more outlines walking in behind him. Who are they? "Boss?" Jagger says quietly, he doesn't seem angry so he must know whoever these people are.

Hudson takes a step backward, he doesn't turn to look at Jagger, his eyes fixated on his opponent. "Jag?"

"Boss, his name is Kevin Lesser, he's a thug who works for anyone who pays him. He has no wife or partner nor does he have any children. His parents are dead and his sister Hayley has disowned him." Jagger informs him, loud enough for only Hudson and I to hear him.

Hudson nods. "Mr Lesser, you're a pitiful fool. No one in your life to care that you're not going to make it through another day."

I finally have a name to put to the face of a monster. Keven Lesser.

Kevin's face drains of all color, the cockiness it once held is long gone and finally the fear is shining through. "How do you know who I am?"

"I know everything, including the fact that your sister Hayley disowned you." The mocking in Hudson's voice makes me feel uncomfortable

There's movement to my left, I know instantly that Harrison is moving closer to me. It's sweet that he's worried but he doesn't need to be, I'm doing okay… for now.

"What do you want from me?" he asks but he already knows the answer to that.

"You're testing my patience, who hired you?" Hudson asks him yet again, although I think he's calmer than he was before he found out who he was.

"I don't understand," Kevin shouts as Jagger advances on him. "Hired me for what?"

"Hired to kidnap two women and keep them in a basement," Jagger tells him and that southern drawl he has is deadly. Both he and Hudson are able to add so much menace to their voices that they take away the men that I know them to be.

Kevin's eyes go wide, he finally connects the dots as to why he's here. "Why?"

I shake my head, that wasn't the right thing to say.

"Why?" Hudson's anger vibrating with every syllable he says. "You kidnapped my woman and you're asking me why I want to know who hired you?"

"What? Your woman?"

Hudson sighs. "Yes, my woman. The gorgeous brunette."

I bite my lip to hide my smile.

"I wasn't told who they were."

My hand reaches out and I connect with Harrison, I squeeze it slightly. "Mia?" He questions, his voice barely above a whisper.

"He's lying, the very first night he told us that the boss would inform us why we were there. Not only that, he said that the boss would be happy that they got two of their girls," I tell him, my voice loud enough for him to hear.

"You're a liar, Kevin, you know exactly who I am. You said that your boss would be happy that you had two of our girls, so how about we try this one last time? Who hired you?" Hudson says through clenched teeth. Christ, Hudson's got impeccable hearing.

Kevin glances around the room. "How did you know that? Where's that bitch?"

The room fills with the sound of bones crunching.

"You do not call my woman a bitch," Hudson yells and it's fucked up but I like this side to him, I find it really sexy.

"I didn't mean your woman, the blonde. She was the only person who could have heard." He's such a weasel, he's trying his best to come across as a badass but in all honesty he's nothing but an asshole.

"That blonde? Her name was Lacey. And because of you she's dead." Jagger's voice calm.

"Dead? No...No, you have it wrong. She's not dead," Kevin mumbles.

"Yes she is. Your boss put two bullets into her and she bled out while my girl held her." Hudson's breathing is getting heavier, he's keeping his distance from Kevin, but I can tell that he wants nothing more than to beat him until all the anger escapes him.

"Liar," he screams.

I step forward unable to listen to anymore of the lies he somehow has made himself believe. "He has hurt people. He hurt Lacey when he pulled that trigger, twice."

Kevin's eyes widen. "You?"

"Yes, me."

"I never hurt you. I looked after you," he tells me and I don't really care if he did or didn't. He fed me, yes, but he took my dignity and every ounce of belief I had. "I looked after you," he repeats as if he's hoping that I'm going to get him out of this.

"Were you the one to render her unconscious when she entered her house?" Hudson grounds out and Kevin's silence is telling.

"So you did hurt her," Jagger says slapping the back of his head.

"I'm sorry," he tells me, he's not sincere and his apology means nothing to me. "But, you're wrong about my boss, he wouldn't have hurt you or your friend."

"He did, he killed Lacey and he didn't even give a shit. Who is he?" I demand, my voice stronger than I thought it would be.

"You're wrong. Why are you lying?" he screams at me, his body lunging forward as if he's trying to reach for me. Jagger's hand clamps down on his shoulder and pulls him back.

I lose it, the bullshit he's spewing out, it's making me so

mad. I'm in a red haze of anger. "I'm not lying and your boss isn't a good man. Good men don't hold people hostage. Good men don't shoot people and good men certainly don't rape people," I yell, each word reverberating off the walls.

"No," He whispers.

"Yes," I reply, my chest heaving as I try and regain my breath.

"Who?" he asks trying to wriggle out of Jagger's hold.

"Me." I'm not afraid anymore, I'm ashamed but not afraid. I hear the deep intakes of breath from the men around the room at my confession. I stand up taller, I'm not letting them see that I'm affected. "Who is it?"

He shakes his head. "I can't."

"Why can't you?" I don't understand, if he said he'd never tell that would be one thing but to say he can't, that just pisses me off.

"Because I can't." He sounds defeated, lost almost.

It's in that moment that I realize why he won't. "You love him, that's why you can't."

He nods, "I'm sorry."

I shake my head. "Don't apologize to me, I don't want nor need your apology. Can you live with yourself knowing that the man you love killed someone? That he raped someone?"

Tears well in his eyes. "I have to believe that he's a good man, that he didn't do those things."

My anger boils once again, this is what I never wanted to happen. Someone to believe that I lied. I take a step closer to him, Hudson's hand reaches out and clamps around my wrist. I'm not to take another step. I grab a hold of his hand and squeeze it like a lifeline. "He did, he grabbed a hold of my leg and pulled me down the mattress. He took my clothes off and no matter how hard I kicked, how hard I begged he wouldn't listen."

"Stop," he begs.

"Yes, that's what I said and he wouldn't stop, he didn't care what I said, what I wanted. He took from me. He hurt me. He pushed inside of me, violating me and he didn't care that he was hurting me, that he took something from me, something I'm never going to get back." I can't stop talking, everything is spilling out of me.

"Stop it."

"Why should I? He never stopped, not until he climaxed, why should I stop to make you feel better? You're hiding a rapist and a killer. Why can't you tell us who it is?"

"I can't," he reiterates.

"Tell me!" I scream at him as Hudson pulls me against his chest.

"Martin," he cries. "His name's Martin Jackson."

Hudson's arms around me convulses. "Martin Jackson?"

I turn in his arms and bury my head against his chest. His arms tightens around me, and I love that he's not pushing me away.

"Yes," Kevin replies. "Do you know him?"

"So you and Martin are a thing?" Jagger asks, disgust in his voice.

"Yes, have been for years. How do you know Martin? Why are you so disgusted? Welcome to the twenty first century." Kevin sounds as though he's in shock.

I'm a bit confused at Jagger, love is love and he shouldn't be disgusted that Martin and Kevin are together.

"You're still protecting the animal, I don't give a fuck if he likes pussy or dick. What I give a fuck about is that he violated a woman that I care about and he shot another."

That's why he's so disgusted, because Martin hurt me, and because Martin has betrayed Hudson.

"What's Martin's plan?" Hudson asks, he's regained his composure. I pull away but he doesn't let me go, he pulls me back against his body.

"I don't know, I haven't spoken to him in a few days." Kevin's lost all the fight he had. He's just a man that's in love and has been used.

"Fine," Hudson growls. "Jagger, take our guest out and bring one of the others in."

Jagger lifts Kevin from the chair and drags him out of the room, as he does he hits the switch and the room's instantly illuminated. I blink harshly as I adjust to the light.

"Leave us," Hudson says and as one the rest of the men leave the room.

"Are you okay?" I ask as soon as we have the room to ourselves.

He laughs. "That's what I was going to ask you. Why wouldn't I be?"

My hands slide up to his face, I frame his head with my fingers. "You just found out that a man you trusted betrayed you. That has to hurt."

He presses a soft kiss against my nose, I tug his head down so that his lips are touching mine. "Princess, I'm done with him, I'm pissed that an innocent man was killed because of the lies he told."

"Who?" The word is out of my mouth before I can stop myself.

"Barney." His answers sounds tortured and it hits me like a tonne of bricks. Barney? Why would he think it was Barney? I don't dare say anything, I can tell he's already regretting his decision in doing so.

"Oh, Hudson," I whisper, lying my head against his

chest. My heart aches for him, knowing that he killed a man he considered a friend.

"I fucked up with Barney but he kept things from me, things didn't add up. He died because he lied when I needed absolute honesty. Martin however is going to die a slow and painful death. What he did to you is unforgivable."

"I love you so much, I wouldn't be this strong without you." It's true, he gives me a strength I didn't know was possible.

"Bullshit." He smirks, "Princess, I'm proud of you, you managed to get that shit out of Kevin. You did so by opening your wound and bleeding. I didn't want that for you."

I kiss him again. "I know you didn't but I didn't bleed, being able to say those words out loud. It healed my wound slightly. We needed to find out who was behind it all and Kevin was never going to tell you."

"I know, if you hadn't spoken he would have died keeping that secret. You're fucking amazing. I'm proud of you, Baby."

I smile, letting his praise soak in. "Thank you."

"When the next man comes in, you don't utter a word. He's a professional and he'll do whatever he can to rile us. That includes you too. So stay hidden and don't say a word."

"I'll stay hidden." I promise him, and step back against the wall.

"Enter," Hudson yells and Harrison walks in and switches the lights off in the room. Once again I'm shrouded in darkness.

FIFTEEN

Hudson
———————

THE LIGHT FLICKERS above this asshole's head, the electricity flowing through his body. We've been at this for two hours and he's still not said a word. Not once has he wavered. It's not a smart move, especially as we already know who has set this up, all I want to know is where Martin is now and what his next move is. I'm sick of being one step behind this fucker, now he's no longer anonymous I'm going to stop him in his tracks. He doesn't know that I have uncovered the truth, there's nowhere for him to hide, I'm coming for him and he's in for a rude awakening once I find him.

Mia has done as I asked and has stayed hidden, this isn't her fight, not now, not with this guy. He'd find her weakness and use it against her. He could break her with mere words, I don't want him to die just yet and if he were to say anything to Mia, I'd lose my damn mind and snap his neck. I'm under no illusion, my weakness is Mia, but at the same time, she's my greatest strength. John Healy walked in with some of his men, he was the person to let me know who Kevin was, it was his way to have a first row seat at what is about to happen. The man is blood thirsty. I was torn between kicking Mia out and fucking her there and then when she started talking, I knew as soon as he saw her that she would be the one to break him.

When she told Kevin that Martin had not only killed but also raped, he didn't believe her. I wanted to put a bullet between his eyes instantly. Everyone present in this room respect rose for her at her announcement that she was the one that was assaulted. She was fucking brave though, she didn't cave, instead she straightened her shoulders and came out fighting. She showed what a true badass she is, she's fucking made for me. She's proven that she's okay with what I do, who I am. There's absolutely no doubt that she's the one for me. It's why I'm no longer waiting around, she's going to be my wife.

Once Jagger turns off the electricity, the man in front of me doesn't seem affected by the hundred-and-twenty voltage that has gone through his body. I know that he's a mercenary, he's trained for this shit. "Are you Martin's side piece?"

Both Jagger and I have known that Martin is bi-sexual, have since we first met him. We never judged him on who he was with. He's a fucking traitor and I need to find out why.

"Go fuck yourself." The fucker spits in Jagger's face and he's rewarded with a punch to his face, the bones crunching beneath Jagger's knuckles.

The way he reacts to being asked if he was Martin's side piece jars something in me, I remember something Martin said to me the day Mia came back into my life.

. . .

"*I want to hire a few guys to come in and protect your family.*"

"*Absolutely not.*" I reply harshly.

"*Listen to me, Boss,*" he implores. "*These guys, they're the best. They're not cops, they don't belong to the government.*"

"*So who are they?*"

"*They're a group of elite men and women. They've been in the military but now are their own company or should I say task force. Look, I don't know much about them other than they're the best and they will make sure your family is safe.*"

"*That's all you got?*" I question.

He lets out a heavy sigh, "*No, my brother, Macka, is part of the team. Boss, the only reason I even know about the team is because of Macka.*"

"*I thought your brother died.*"

"*Yeah boss, you're finally getting why they're the best.*"

"*How long has this team being going? What do they specialize in?*" I ask, wanting to find out as much as I can.

"*Um...*" He wavers, "*That I'm not entirely sure of, I've not long found out he's still alive.*"

They're mercenaries, that's what they are. "*I'll let you know, in the meantime talk to Barney and let him know what the situation is. Tell him to keep his ear close to the ground. I'll be arriving there tonight and I'll be bringing Jagger and you with me.*"

"Macka?" I question and his head pops up, his eyes wide as if he's been caught out. Yes, that's right fucker, I know who you are.

"Macka?" Jagger spits in disgust. He knows who Macka is. "It must be a fucking riot at family get togethers. What with you being a ghost and your brother a traitor."

Macka pulls against his restraints. "He's not a traitor," he yells, his face red with anger.

Jagger pulls on Macka's hair, his head flies backward. "That's where you're wrong. Your brother is a traitor. He has hurt innocent women, he killed a woman for no reason other than pleasure. He took Hudson's woman. He's a dead man walking. He's betrayed our boss, the man that trusted him."

"Why should he be the boss? Why should he have everything when Martin has nothing?" Macka yells, anger lacing his words.

"I'm the boss because it's what I have been destined to be since birth. Just as my father was. I am the son of the boss, the grandson of the original Kingpin. There was no one else to be the boss."

He smirks, as if he knows something I don't. "That's not entirely true. You want to know the truth, you should look a lot closer to home."

I advance on him, this cloak and dagger bullshit doesn't fly with me. If you have something to say, spit it the fuck out. "How about you just tell me?" I grind out.

The look in his eyes tell me he's never going to answer me. He'd rather die than betray his brother. With Hulk like strength, he escapes his restraints and within the blink of an eye reaches for his ankle, my teeth clench when I see the glistening of the gun barrel. "Jagger." I growl but it's too late, he's already got the gun in his mouth.

"No," I hear the tiny whisper, but it's too late.

Bang.

Blood splatters everywhere, as his body hits the floor. "Who the fuck let him in with a gun?" My anger palpable. "Check the fucking others." My nostrils flare as I try and keep my composure, I'm close to ending everyone in this room for their incompetence. "Now!"

The men scramble out of the room, leaving Mia, Jagger, my dad and I alone. Dad switches on the light and Macka's body comes into view.

"Hudson…" Dad begins but I hold my hand up stopping him. My eyes are focused on Mia, she can't stop staring at Macka's body. "Mia, are you okay?" he asks, realizing why I stopped him talking.

She nods, unable to tear her gaze away, "Why did he do that? He could have done it at the very beginning, but why did he wait until then?" She sounds perplexed, is she staring at him as she's curious of his motives or is she staring at him because he's dead. Maybe it's a mixture of the two?

"Mia, he was cornered, they always take the easiest way out," Jagger tells her softly.

I stand in front of her and instantly her eyes lift to mine. "Princess?"

"He had the gun the entire time he was here Hudson, he was cornered. Why didn't he do it before?" She muses out loud, I let her be, let her get out whatever is playing on her mind. "Macka seemed to believe that you wouldn't find Martin, or why he's doing this. That was until he slipped up. He said something he shouldn't have and killed himself."

"Okay and how did he slip up?" I ask, I can see what she's saying, I'm just not entirely sure that she's right.

"I don't know, but I think it has to do with what he said. When Jagger called Martin a traitor, something in Macka seemed to switch. He said, 'Why should Hudson be the boss? Why should Hudson have everything when Martin has nothing?'"

"Mia, I think you're stretching here," Jagger says softly and my eyes cut to his, warning him to tread carefully.

She shakes her head. "I don't think I am, see when

Hudson explained that he is the only heir to the kingdom, there was no one else to be boss, Macka said it wasn't true, that Hudson needed to look a lot closer to home."

He fucking did say that. "Princess, what are you saying?"

She turns to face my father. "Harrison, you know what Macka was hinting at, don't you." It's not a question but a statement.

"Dad?" I ask, wondering where the hell this is going. He glances to the floor and it pisses me off. "Dad, do you want to tell me what the fuck is going on?" I say through clenched teeth.

He sighs heavily. "Look son, I made a mistake, one that seems to be biting me in the ass now."

I raise my brow, what the fuck is that supposed to mean?

"I was fifteen and I thought with my dick as most boys do at that age. I got a married woman pregnant. I told the woman to go back to her husband, I wasn't going to marry her and if she told anyone about our affair, I'd have her killed," he says with no emotion at all and Mia gasps at his honesty.

He gives her a tight smile. "I wasn't joking, I had a lot of growing up to do but I was too young for a fucking kid. She went back to her husband, he never knew that his second child wasn't his. I had nothing to do with that child, no one besides my dad knew and he kept tabs on him. Making sure that he was brought up right."

"Martin is your son," I say with utter disgust.

He nods. "Yes, your grandfather wanted him to be a part of the family business when he was eighteen. I didn't agree, I didn't think he deserved to be part of this. I had you, you are my son. My only son," he spits, as if that makes everything okay.

"Dad, you're a fucking asshole. You don't think you should have told me this before? I mean you had the bastard being my chauffeur since I was fifteen. I let that fucker work his way to my second in command."

"Son, I know..."

"You know nothing!" I scream cutting him off, "You let me bring that bastard around Mia." My own fucking brother raped my woman. I'm going to rip his head off.

"Son..." he doesn't continue, he has no words. I don't want to hear any of them anyway.

"Where is he, Dad?" There's no more playing, now I know why he's doing this shit, it's time to fucking end it.

"I don't know. I haven't been able to locate him."

I lose it, a red haze darkens over me. Hands go around me and I beat them away, not even sure who it was but I'm advancing toward Dad. He knows what's about to happen and he doesn't move. He stands his ground, waiting for what's about to come. I pull my arm back, balling my hand into a fist and letting it fly. My knuckles connecting with his cheek, the sound of skin hitting skin satisfies my inner beast.

"Hudson, that's it man," Jagger says, his hands gripping my arms, pulling me back.

I shrug him off, that haze disappearing. I stand and stare at the man that has always managed to disappoint. He has no fucking morals whatsoever.

"You good now?" he asks with a smirk.

"Nowhere even close," I snap back and his eyes narrow. "You fucking knew it was him and you didn't do a thing. You never said." My anger is beginning to rise. He has fucked up more times than I can count, but this. God, knowing that Martin did this and not saying anything, especially after finding out what he did to Mia, pisses me off. I could kill him and I'd be happy with my decision. I'd walk away smiling.

He steps forward, Jagger tenses behind me. "Don't. I would never put you or Mia in danger. I didn't know, I had a suspicion and that's all it was." His voice vibrating with anger, "I may be an asshole, Hudson, but not to you, everyone else maybe. You are my son, I'd die for you."

"You're a..."

"Enough!" Mia shouts cutting me off which has me turning to look at her only to find her sitting on the floor. I take a step toward her, but she shakes her head. "Don't."

"Mia?" I question, what the hell?

"You're a jerk!" she shouts getting to her feet. "You pushed me over! Can we stop the arguments?"

Fuck, it was her that I pushed past. "Princess, I'm sorry."

She shakes her head. "Its fine, I know that you didn't mean it. Look, there's no point in arguing, we need to be a team right now. Being at each other's throats is only helping *him*."

I walk over to her, she's been through so much pain and violence that the last thing she needs is to be pushed over by me or to listen to me going in on my dad. Pulling her into my arms, she comes willingly. "How the hell are you always right?" I quip kissing her head.

"Get used to it," Dad laughs. "You've found yourself a good one son, don't let her go."

I give him a hard stare, he has no idea how to treat a woman. "I've no intention of letting her go."

"So, what's the plan now?" Mia questions, looking between us all. I take her in, her eyes are heavy and her arms are around her stomach almost as if she's protecting herself. She looks tired.

"They're not going to talk, they're trained for this shit," Dad says. "End them all and let's get out of here."

"Your dad's right, Hudson, end them and leave them on Martin's doorstep. Show him, that we know he's responsible and we're coming for him." Jagger's drawl is full of anger. I'm not the only one he's betrayed, he's done it to all my men, my family. He's played us all for a fucking long time. This wouldn't have happened if dad had been honest or kept that fucker away from us.

I nod, time to put this into action. "Jagger, sort it out. The Healy's are here to give you a hand if you need too. Dad, find out where that fucker is. I have to inform my men that there's a traitor among them. Take him out of here, those outside will be wondering what's happened, they'll realize they've fucked up when they see his body."

"What about me? What am I doing?" She sounds worried.

"You're going home to bed." I give her a look, telling her not to argue with me. "Princess, you look ready to drop."

She pouts but nods. "Fine. Although I don't know if I'll be able to. But may as well try." She walks toward the door, her head held high but I can tell by the way she's holding herself that it's not fine. She's scared.

"Princess?" I ask as I wrap my fingers around her wrist, stopping her from walking. I glance at Dad and Jagger and nod my head toward the door, telling them to leave. They don't hang around, both giving Mia an encouraging squeeze on her shoulder. Jagger lifts Macka's body over his shoulder and they both leave Mia and I alone. "What's wrong?"

She shrugs. "What if he gets me again?" It's whisper, one that's laced with fear and pain.

"That's not going to happen. My house is locked up

tighter than fort Knox. No one is getting in unless it's me. Even Jagger can't get in. When I realized that I had a traitor, I changed all codes, added better locks, and changed the camera positioning's. If someone is within twenty-five meters of my house, an alarm will be sent to my phone and I'll be able to see who it is. You're safe there Mia."

Her hands go to my chest, as she stands on her tiptoes and presses a kiss against my lips. "I love you so much. Thank you," she whispers.

"Don't thank me, Princess, I'm doing what I have to so that you're safe. Without you I'm nothing." She smiles, there's absolutely no fear in her eyes at all, she's believes me. This is it. "You're gonna marry me," I tell her.

Her smile drops. "What?"

"You heard me, Mia. You're going to marry me."

She blinks… Once, twice, three times. "Is that your way of asking?"

"Mia, I love you and you love me. Do you see yourself with anyone else?" I give her a hard stare.

She frowns, taking a step away from me. "No."

"Then you're going to marry me."

Her lips twist into a smile. "Fine, yes, I'm going to marry you."

I smile, who knew getting engaged would make me feel relieved? "Good, I'll get it set up."

"I'm sorry?" She questions her teeth capturing her bottom lip.

"What?"

She places her hands on her hip, "Hudson Brady, did we just get engaged?"

I throw my arm around her waist and pull her toward me. "Yes."

"No ring, no getting down on bended knee? Just 'you're going to marry me.'"

"Yeah baby. Don't worry, you'll have a ring." I kiss her lips, a calm feeling settling over me.

She huffs. "God, you're such a caveman."

"No, I just know what I want. And that's you."

A smile brightens up her face. "You have such a way with words."

"Love you, Princess." My hand tangles in her hair, my lips capture hers, my tongue invades her mouth, the kiss deepens and I direct her toward the wall. Her hands roaming my body. I need her, it's been too long since I've been inside of her. I tear my mouth away from her.

"Don't," she gasps, "I want this. I need this." She tells me as her hands go to my pants. "Hudson," she says, her chest rapidly rising and falling. "I love you, I need you like I need air. Don't treat me like I'm fragile."

My hands goes to the hem of her dress and pushes it up. My fingers go to her panties and I pull them off her, needing to be inside of her as quickly as possible.

"Hurry," she begs as she pushes down my pants, my dick as hard as rock. She whimpers when she sees it.

My hands go to her ass cheeks and I lift her, positioning my dick at the entrance to her vagina. I don't even hesitate in pushing inside of her. She gasps as I fill her. I pull out of her, and she whimpers, her hands grabbing at my shirt pulling me closer to her. When I push inside of her, it feels fucking amazing, I'm bare inside of her wet, hot pussy. My mouth attacks her, needing to dominate every inch of her at once. She doesn't even protest, she gives me all of her, every single piece of her is mine and I take it with no mercy. Thrusting inside of her harder and harder each time, my pleasure climbing higher and higher with every movement.

Mia's groans with each thrust and I know that I'm not the only one that's close. "Hudson. Oh, Hudson. Please," she begs and I give it to her. I thrust so hard into her that she hits against the wall, I don't stop, the pounding is hard and frantic but the sounds coming from her aren't in fear, they're in want. She's mine and I can't wait to show her just how fucking amazing fucking can truly be. I've been soft with her now, it's changing. She's mine, she's more than proven that.

I thrust into her once more, and she detonates, screaming my name as she comes. Her pussy contracts around my dick, pulling my come from me. I groan as I cum, unloading inside of her.

"Fuck, Mia," I growl as I kiss her neck, her legs wrapped around my waist, my dick still inside of her. I'd love nothing more than to fuck her again, but it's time to go, I've people waiting and shit to do. "Once I get home, I'm going to fuck you all night long. You're not going to be able to move by the time I'm finished with you." I promise her.

She laughs. "Sounds delicious." Her tongue snakes out and wets her lips

She's fucking dirty and I love it. "Made for me," I tell her and her eyes light up. "I love you, Princess."

She melts into me. "I love you, too." Then she squeals, "We're getting married!"

"Yep, now we've got to go." I do the zipper up on my pants as she smooths out her dress. Once we're both ready, I take her hand and we leave the room, both my dad and Jagger waiting for me as we exit. Jagger has a smirk on his face, and I shoot him a dark look. He better not even open his damn mouth.

SIXTEEN

Mia

Two weeks later

"HUDSON, DO I LOOK OKAY?" I ask standing in front of the mirror. My black dress hanging off me, I've lost a lot of weight. My hair is straight and falls down my back, I've a pair of small white gold diamond studs in my ears, they match the ring Hudson bought for me. He came home the night he told me I was marrying him with this huge pear cut engagement ring. It's the most gorgeous ring I've ever seen, Hudson told me it's a twenty-six karat diamond. I cried when he placed it on my finger. I still can't believe that I'm engaged, but I'm happy that I am. I love Hudson with all my heart and marrying him means that I get to spend the rest of my life with him.

"You look beautiful," he replies softly, I look through the mirror and see him standing, watching me. He looks handsome, everything about him is clean and neat. From his perfectly pressed black suit, to his impeccably polished shoes. There's not a hair out of place either.

He glances at me, he's worried, he told me before we flew out here that I hadn't grieved for Lacey, he thinks I'm going to fall apart now that we're here and going to her funeral. I may sob, I may crumble to the ground as the pain hits me that she's really gone, but I won't break. Martin will not break me, I'm not going to let him ruin my life any more than he already has. He took Lacey's life, he took Barney's life, and I won't let him take anymore.

"Do you think mom's here?" She told me she'd come but when Hudson was booking the flights she told us she'd get her own way here. I appreciate that Jagger and Harrison are here.

Sarah wanted to come but we all agreed it was too risky, especially now we know that it's Martin that's after us. None of us want her or Allie in danger. I wouldn't put it past Martin to hurt either of them for his stupid vendetta. We still have no idea where he is, he's gone to ground and everyone's efforts are focused on finding him. I don't think he'll be found until he wants to be, he managed to keep being Hudson's brother quiet for over fifteen years, it shows he's good at hiding things.

"I don't know, Dad called her earlier but there was no answer."

I think they've split up, no one is saying anything but Harrison has been staying at Hudson's and Mom's been staying in a motel. Whenever Mom comes to the house Harrison either leaves the room or leaves the house.

I glance at my watch, it's time to leave, and the car should be downstairs waiting for us. "We should go." I don't want to but I know that I have too. She was my best friend, my sister. I feel as though a piece of me is missing. I've buried it deep down, not wanting to feel the pain that comes whenever someone says her name, whenever I hear *I took a pill in Ibiza by Mike Posner*. It was our jam, whenever it would come on, we'd sing it at the top of our lungs. Now whenever I hear it, my eyes well with tears and I want to crawl into a corner and sob.

"Yeah, Princess, we should leave." He walks over to me and pulls me into his arms. I rest my head against his chest, my hands going around his waist, and I inhale his scent. He smells minty, he's just brushed his teeth. "Ready?" he asks after a couple of minutes and I nod, not wanting to let go of him. I reach for my sunglasses and put them on, it'll hide the tears once they fall.

As soon as we leave our hotel room, I spot Harrison and Jagger standing by the elevator. I wonder how long they've been standing there. They're always waiting for us, I feel bad in case they've been there for a long time. Whenever I ask, I always get the same answers, not long, or it's their job. Everyone looks sombre, both Harrison and Jagger offer me a small, sad smile, one that I return. Hudson's hand grips mine, offering me support as we step into the elevator.

The elevator doors close, no one says a word. What is there to say? Lacey's gone and she's never coming back, Martin's still out there and we have no idea where he is or what he has planned next. Every time Hudson leaves the house I worry that I'll never see him again. It's something that I have to get used to. Hudson is always going to have enemies, he'll always piss someone off, it's the nature of his career. While I don't condone him selling drugs, I have said that I'll stand behind him. I'm not going to change him, or what he does. There is only one thing I've asked and that is he be one hundred percent honest with me. If something's happening, I want to know, I don't want to be in the dark about it. He's agreed saying that it's going to be total honesty with us, although he won't go into details about the people he works with or the things he does, anything that leads to danger he'll tell me.

The elevator dings, and the doors slide open. Instantly I see, Aaron, Greg, David, and Liam. They're Hudson's men, they've proven to Hudson that they're not working for Martin and that they're loyal to him. They're all strapped, at least two guns on each of them, I can see the outline of it on Aaron's back. He has it hidden under his suit jacket, although not that hidden. I glance at Harrison, checking to see if he too has a gun. If he does, he has it well concealed.

Walking through the hotel lobby, the hair on the back of my neck stands up, someone's watching me. Glancing around, trying to see whose making me feel this way.

"Princess?" Hudson asks, his eyes narrowed.

I don't see anyone, maybe I'm imagining things? "It's nothing." I brush him off, "Has anyone heard from Mom?"

Hudson exchanges a look with someone behind me, whatever they're silently conveying doesn't look good. "Dad's going to call her and see where she is. She's probably waiting for us at the church."

I nod. "Yeah, you're probably right." I don't think she is, I just have a knot in the pit of my stomach, something is going on with her and I need to know what. She's tried her hardest since I've been home to make things right, but she just can't keep her disdain for Hudson to herself. Hudson, being Hudson makes sure she knows that her disrespect is noted and that she's skating on thin ice. He hasn't done anything yet because of me.

As soon as we're outside the men gather around us. "Aaron and Greg, you're in the lead car, David and Liam, you're trailing us," Hudson instructs and the men instantly nod. "Jagger, you're driving."

Jagger smirks. "Told you old man," he taunts Harrison.

Since Hudson and I got engaged, things between him and his dad have eased, they're getting along better and Hudson doesn't want to kill him. Harrison seems to have mellowed out a bit too, especially while staying in Hudson's house, he's always joking with the men, something Hudson told me he never did before. Jagger even teases him, telling that he's got better with age. I think because Jagger has been a part of their family for a long time, he's able to get away with it. None of the other men dare to say anything.

Hudson's mom hasn't been by, she won't while Harrison's in the house, I totally understand that and have told him that we could go to her house once we get back. I can't wait to meet her, from everything Hudson's told me she's really worked hard to find who she is. He told me that while his parents were married, that his mom lost a sense of who she was. She's moving on, I'm secretly hoping that she finds someone who'll treat her like a queen, just as her son treats me.

I slide into the back of the car, Hudson following right behind me, I glance down at my watch, its 10:40 am, there's only twenty minutes until the service starts, I don't want to be late. I can't miss her funeral. The car starts and Jagger pulls off toward the church.

"We'll be there in fifteen minutes," Hudson says and I give him a smile, he always seems to know what to say to reassure me.

"Thanks." I reach for his hand and intertwine my fingers with his. I sink into the seat and turn to look out the window, watching everyone we pass, they all seem so happy and unaware of the evils that occurs every day. I watch children chasing one another and wonder if Hudson and I will ever be able to have that? Will our child be able to live a relatively normal life like I had? Or will they be destined to be Kingpin just as their father was? I guess that's a conversation for another day.

"We're here," Jagger announces as he parks a little bit down from the church.

Relief washes through me, I'm not going to miss it. I reach for the car door handle and open it, wanting to get some fresh air into me.

"Mia," Hudson growls. "Wait for us to exit first." This is the third time that he's said this to me, it's something I'm not used to, waiting until it's safe.

"Sorry," I mumble feeling like a child that's been scolded.

He gets out of the car and walks around to my side. He opens the door and holds out his hand for me to take. "You've got to remember this Mia, anyone could be waiting to ambush us."

I roll my eyes. "I know, I said I was sorry." I climb out of the car and look around, so many faces that I don't know. I don't see Lacey's parents anywhere, maybe they're inside the church already.

"I didn't think you were going to make it on time." My eyes widen when I hear that raspy voice. A smile forms on my lips and I turn around. "Always the way with you though Mia. You can never be early."

I raise my brow. "Coming from the woman that can't do anything she's asked. What are you doing here Sarah? We told you it was safer to stay in New York." God, it's so good to see her. "Where's Allie?"

She nods her head to the left, a beautiful smile graces her face. Standing by the gate is Sarah's brother Frankie who's holding onto Allie's stroller. "He got back last week, he called me and I told him everything. He flew to New York and has been staying with me, when I told him I wanted to come to Lacey's funeral he made sure I'd be here."

I release Hudson's hand and walk over to her, she opens her arms and I fall into them. "God, I'm so glad you disobeyed orders," I whisper as my arms wrap around her.

"Me too, I couldn't stay away. She was my friend Mia, she helped me out and I'd never forgive myself if I didn't come." Wetness hits my shoulder and I tighten my hold on her, showing her that she's not alone. "Mia, how are you holding up?"

I pull away from her. "I'm doing better." It's not a lie, my frame of mind is better. I can't sleep with the light off, so Hudson has the en-suite light shining so if I wake up, I'm not shrouded in darkness.

"Liar," she mouths but her eyes light up, looking at where her gaze is focused. Frankie and Allie are walking over to us. "He's been such a help, I didn't realize how much I had missed him."

"I bet, even I missed him. What was his reaction to Allie?" I'd say he was shocked to say the least.

"At first he was angry that I didn't tell him. But he soon got over that and he's besotted with her."

As soon as Frankie's close, I walk over to him. His smile grows and he opens his arms out wide, "Missed me, huh?"

I ignore him and look down at the beauty in her stroller. "Hello Allie, I've missed you so much." I unbuckle her, ignoring the laughter coming from the guys and the grumble from Frankie. Lifting Allie out, I hold her close to me, I inhale her scent, there's something about the smell of a baby that just makes everything better. "You're the cutest girl ever," I whisper placing a kiss on her chubby little cheek.

"Seriously?" Frankie whines and I laugh.

"Get it through your head, you are no longer second best, you've been relegated." Sarah quips.

I walk over to Sarah, Hudson, and Jagger. Both Hudson and Jagger have been staring at me since I picked up Allie, both for very different reasons, although I have no idea what that look in Hudson's eyes is. I'd love to hand Allie over to Jagger but I think that's something that Sarah should do. "She's gotten so big," I remark as I hand her to her mom.

"You're telling me, I blink and she's grown a couple of inches." She kisses Allie's head and Jagger inches closer to them.

I turn my attention to Frankie and Hudson. "Frankie, meet Hudson." I smile, he's still not happy that I haven't hugged him. "Hudson, this is Sarah's brother, Frankie."

"Hey," Hudson says with an edge to his tone.

I walk over to Frankie and hug him. "Thanks for coming, I know you never got the chance to meet Lace, but she'd have loved you," I say as I pull back and smile at him.

"What's not to love," he quips and I smack his shoulder. "No, in all seriousness, Sarah told me about her, about what you both did for her and Allie. I'm forever in your debt."

I wave my hand in dismissal. "No you're not, Sarah's my best friend, has been for years. She's like a sister."

His eyes narrow in on my hand. "You're engaged?" He sounds shocked, pissed even.

Hudson steps closer to me, his hand on the base of my back. "Yes, I am." My tone less than pleased.

"I'm sorry, it was a surprise, Sarah never said anything."

I know why he's angry, Sarah's obviously told him about who Hudson is. I told her everything about Jagger and Hudson, with their permission of course, and she wasn't as shocked as I thought she'd be. We spoke about everything that happened, I told her everything except for what Martin did to me. I just can't bring myself to tell her, I don't want the pity, or things to change between us. She doesn't treat me like I'm fragile and I don't want that to change. I don't want her to think I'm weak.

"Mia, we should go in," Hudson says breaking the awkwardness. His hand pressing against my back, directing me forward.

"I'm sorry, I'm an ass. Congratulations." Frankie holds out his hand for him to shake and it's then that I realize he never replied to Hudson when he said *hi* to him.

"Thanks," Hudson says quickly shaking his hand. This is awkward and now isn't the time.

I reach for Hudson's hand, and turn to Sarah, Jagger's holding Allie, his eyes so full of love as he looks at his daughter. "I'm going to go and find a seat," I tell her, and Jagger glances up at me and winks. I blow him a kiss and Hudson pulls me into his body.

She nods. "Yeah, I'm coming too."

"You okay, Princess?"

I lean my head against his shoulder as we wait for Jagger and Sarah to get Allie back in her stroller. "I'm okay, I've really missed her and even though we said for her not to come. I'm glad she did."

"Jagger's happy she's here too." He kisses my head. "It's time to go in." His mood turns sombre, and I glance to the church, everyone is making their way inside. I tentatively take a step forward, my chest burns with pain.

An arm links through mine and I know without looking that it's Sarah. "Let's go do this and then when it's over, let's get drunk."

"God, yes," I breathe. One step at a time, one foot in

front of the other. It's all I can do right now. I've buried this deep down and now it's finally coming to the surface. Having both Hudson and Sarah here for support means the world, I have someone to lean on, have someone who's going through the same.

As soon as I enter the church, I look around, no Mom. She didn't come. I shouldn't be surprised but I am. I'm deeply hurt that she's not here. I take my seat, Hudson and Sarah flanking either side of me. A tear falls and it's like the floodgates have opened, and they cascade down my face as I mouth the words I wish I could say to her.

I love you Lacey, I'm sorry I couldn't protect you.

SEVENTEEN

Hudson

ONE WEEK LATER

"MOM, LEAVE HER ALONE," I roll my eyes as I walk into the house.

She looks good, every time I see her, she looks happier. Each time I look at her or talk to her she seems better. No longer depressed, or allowing the past to get to her. She's not living in my father's shadow or focusing on me. She's working on herself and its showing, she's smiling, she finally has that twinkle in her eyes and I'm guessing it means she's dating again.

"Oh hush you. I've been dying to meet Mia. You've finally brought her with you." She holds Mia at arm's length, giving her a once over. "You're too skinny you need to eat. It's a good thing I have food ready for you. Let's get you some."

Mia's eyes widen as Mom grabs her arm and leads her into the house. I can't help but smile, I don't think I've ever seen Mia as nervous as she is right now. She shouldn't be worried, Dad loves her which surprised the crap out of me, and I didn't think he was capable of loving anyone. Mom's going to love her, because I do. It's that simple.

My cell rings and I look down to see Jagger's name flashing on the screen. What the hell is he calling me for? He's meant to be spending time with Sarah and Allie. "I've got to take this," I tell them and Mia immediately tenses as she does each time my phone rings.

"Go, Son, I've got our girl." She assures me and I nod. She will, she'll ensure she's safe. Dad had Mom trained, he wanted to make sure that she knew how to protect me along with herself.

I walk back outside, knowing that Mia's okay. "What's up?"

"Boss, we've got a fucking problem," he says through clenched teeth, a baby crying in the background

"Talk to me," I demand. What the fuck has happened now?

He sighs, whatever is about to come out of his mouth isn't good. Jagger always sighs when there's bad news. It's a tell he has, it also means I brace myself for what he's about to say. "Aaron just called me. David's house has just been firebombed."

"Shit. Anyone inside?" I ask, my mind immediately goes to Martin, would that fucker have done this? Of course he would have.

"His wife was inside. David is at hospital now with her. Boss, it's not looking good. Aaron said at least seventy percent of her body is burnt, she's barely breathing, and she's in a lot of pain. They don't reckon she's going to survive the night, and if she does it'll be touch and go whether her body can fight off an infection if she gets one, not to mention all the skin grafts she's going to have to have along with the surgeries. They're not optimistic at all."

"Who?" I ask, even though I already know.

"Martin." One word contains so much hate, and so much anger.

"How do you know it's him? Was it actually him, or is it someone else doing his dirty work?" I can't believe this fucker is still one step ahead that he's always still managing to screw with everyone around me.

"Yes it was him. One hundred percent. Seems as though he has no one left to do his dirty work. What the bastard didn't know is that David had a new system put in. He wanted to ensure his family was safe. He caught that fucker on camera."

Fuck! "Get every CCTV camera from around the area, I want to know what car he was driving and where the fuck he's heading. This ends Jag, this ends real soon. I want that bastard six feet under."

"We're going to get him, Boss. He's making mistakes now, too many." The determination is clear to hear.

Yes he is, he got sloppy, he must have thought no one would talk. How wrong he was. Now he has no one to help him. The problem with being sloppy? You get reckless, and that means more deaths and more intensity. He's not finished yet. I have no idea what his endgame is but I can hazard a guess… he wants me to die.

"He is and that means we have to be extra vigilant, we have to be alert. We have no idea what this fucker's next play is. Spread the word, everyone is to be on alert. All family to be moved to a safe house. You know where." We discussed this only yesterday, only me and Jagger know where to move the families. It's the way it's going to stay. Now my men have seen what Martin will do to their families, there's no way they'd not send their families away to ensure their safety.

"The men have already been informed, all of them want Martin's blood. He's lost the trust of all the men.

There's no way they would believe that he is being set up, they've seen the evidence, all the men were at the hospital when David showed them the video…"

I cut him off. "Why wasn't I called beforehand?" I should have been informed as soon as it happened.

"Boss, that's my fault. This is Mia's chance at meeting your mom, you're engaged now, Boss, I know this means a lot to Mia. The girl has been through enough, she just wants normality."

What the hell? "Jesus fucking Christ, you've been listening to Sarah." I laugh, someone's taken his damn balls.

"Shut up!" he growls. "The men have seen the footage, they know he is responsible. There's no hiding from this. Before there was a slight doubt, that maybe he too was being set up like Barney had been. Now we all know that Martin set Barney up, and Barney paid the price. No one is setting Martin up, he's doing this on his own for his own benefit. He's well and truly fucked there's no coming back from this…"

"No, there was no coming back when he stole my woman, there was no coming back when he raped her. There is no coming back full stop," I say through clenched teeth, pissed off at his choice of wording.

"Boss, I didn't mean it like that…"

"I don't care how you meant it. I'm telling you now there was no way he was coming back at all. No matter who he's killed. The acts he's committed have proved that. The things he did to Mia, he took the lives of Lacey and Barney. That's too much, I don't forgive and I certainly won't be forgiving him." Jagger needs to shut the hell up, the man is making my anger rise.

"I'm going to be quiet now because I just keep putting my foot in my mouth. You know that I love Mia and I will do anything for her, I'd give my life to protect her. I would have done the same for Lacey. But she paid the ultimate price. I have so much guilt at not being able to get to her in time. So much guilt for not seeing what Martin was. That eats away at me every single day. I was one of the closest to him and I didn't see the truth behind that facade. I'm grateful, it's selfish but I am grateful that Sarah wasn't there, because no doubt if they had been in California, she would have been at that house with Lacey and Mia, then she too would have been taken." His voice cracks at just the thought of it.

"It's not selfish. I still need to find out how he knew where Mia would be that day. The only thing I can think of is that he's had her phone tapped, traced, or some techy shit like that. He got lucky in the sense that Lacy was there too, and yes if Sarah had been there he probably would have taken her as well. You and I both know that our women mean everything, without them we are nothing, and with them we are stronger. If you take them away from us, you make an enemy for life, hurt them and you die. It's the way of life, it's the way things have to be and not only did Martin take her, he hurt her in ways that she will never be able to recover from. And for that he'll pay the ultimate price."

A jagged breath escapes him. "Boss, I know. But I also know that we have to be smart about this because as much as we like to think we know Martin and what he's going to do, we don't."

It's something I've known for a while, something I've been thinking about and I finally know how to do it. "I know Jag, I know. That's why we are going to have to take a step back. We're going to find out everything there is to know about Martin, search for every single detail of his life and find out what he could have planned next. Right now we are sitting ducks, waiting for him to take out one of us. We are in limbo and it's got to stop."

"We'll call a meeting, have every man on it," he tells me, but it won't work.

"No, I have someone on it already." My dad, I've told him to give me every detail of Martin's life. As much as he's an asshole, he actually gives a shit about Mia and I and that's why he'll always have our backs.

"Hudson…" he begins, and I know that he's going to ask something, he always says my name if he wants to talk to me frankly. "Do you think you can trust him?"

"Do I trust that he's turned his back on Martin?" I ask trying to clarify what he means.

"Yes, Martin is his son too," he tells me something I already know.

"No, I don't, but I do think he'll do what's right and as I'm the boss, his loyalty is with me." That I can say with absolute faith.

"Good, we don't need him having help from anyone else."

"Dad wouldn't do that," I reiterate.

"Hudson, are you certain?"

Fuck. "If he turns his back on me, then I won't hesitate to put a bullet in his head."

"Me either. You know what they say, keep your friends close…"

"Your enemies closer. Yeah I know and believe me Jag, I've got him closer than I've ever had him before."

He makes a tutting noise. "Yeah, I know that, Boss, but he's also got you closer than ever."

I can't believe this shit. This is my dad, the man's meant to have loyalty to me. "I'm going to go, I'll swing by the hospital once I have Mia home."

"Okay, Boss, call me if you need me."

"Will do, talk to you later, need to rescue my girl before mom frightens her off."

He laughs. "No chance boss. Mia loves you."

"She was made for me, Jag." She really was, I never expected to find a woman who would be so fucking strong.

"Definitely was, just as Sarah was for me."

"Okay, enough of this shit. I've gotta go." I end the call and sigh, fucking Martin. He's the bane of my existence.

I know that Mia still has trouble sleeping if I'm not in bed beside her. If I have to work late or even leave the house during the middle of the night, whenever I come back, she'll be in the living room watching telly. Even if I am in bed with her, she still has to have the light on.

Walking back into the house, I hear laughter. I stand at the door and watch as the two women I care about most in this world, laugh as though they have no troubles.

"Has Hudson always been so…" Mia trails off as if she's trying to find the right word.

"So intense?" Mom laughs.

"Yes!" Mia cries. "Hudson's been intense from the moment I met him. He just had this air of intensity and mystery about him. I've been drawn to him from the very beginning. He's so bossy and direct." Mia bites her lip, it's what she does if she's worried.

"Hudson is direct, just as his father is, and no doubt just as I am. We get straight to the point, because there's no sense in beating around the bush with a hundred words, when you can say one. With Hudson, the intensity he has with you is different, his intense stems from his love. It's obvious to see that he loves you, it's clear to see just by one look. I've never seen my son so… in love." Mom smiles, she likes Mia and Mia's comfortable around her.

"But the intensity he has with you, is his drive and his need to ensure your safety. Mia, when you were taken

Hudson was a wreck, it was that moment that I know that Hudson had found the woman for him. My son doesn't become a wreck, he is the boss, and he needs to show his strength and his power. But when a man finds a woman they truly love, that woman becomes their greatest weakness," Mom tells her and it's not malicious, she's informing Mia, from the wife of a boss to another. Or soon to be.

"Weakness?" Mia whispers sounding horrified.

Mom reaches over and grasps Mia's hand. "Weakness. It's not a bad thing Mia, you're his weakness - not in the sense that you are making him weak but in a way that if any of his enemies wanted to hurt him, the quickest way to do so is by hurting you. But while you are his weakness, you are his greatest strength, just as it should be, Mia. Do not over think it, it is what it is and there's nothing you can do about it except be vigilant if you are out without a man on your back. Although, I doubt that will ever happen."

I smile, she's preparing her, informing her of everything I would never.

"This is how I knew that Harrison wasn't the man I had always believed he was. "I was the mother of his child, he would have done anything to protect me. I wasn't the woman he loved." Mom tells her honestly, a hint of sadness in her tone, and Mia gasps, her eyes filling with tears.

Mom shakes her head. "Mia, it's okay, it was hard but I'm okay about it now."

"Did you know about his other son?" Mia asks softly and I tense, I haven't said anything to Mom about Martin.

"I did know. It also wasn't my place to say anything to Hudson. Harrison had a secret and it was his secret to tell. He promised me that Hudson nor I would ever have to deal with Martin or Martin's family, that he had no intention of being a dad to him or inviting Martin into our family. I knew that Hudson's grandfather Henry wanted Martin close. Henry was all about family and he didn't agree with Harrison's decision not to have Martin part of his life."

"Henry?" Mia laughs.

Mom rolls her eyes. "Yes, Henry, Harrison, and Hudson. If you ever have a son Mia, you'll be expected to name him something beginning with an H."

Something flashes through Mia's eyes but I'm not sure what it is but as quick as it was there, it disappears.

"In the end it was Harrison's decision and it was a decision that I fully supported. By the time Harrison and I got married and we had Hudson, Martin was older and he was in with a bad crowd to be quite honest and it was something that I didn't want Hudson to be around it was also something that Harrison didn't tolerate, the family didn't tolerate it." Mom explains and I understand why she wanted it to be a secret, but I still can't believe that they managed to keep it quiet for over thirty years.

I step out of the shadows. "So how did he become part of the family?" I ask, knowing that I'm going to get an honest answer from mom.

"Jesus son, you scared the life out of me!" Mom cries placing a hand on her chest, her other hand still holding onto Mia's. She takes one look at my face and realise I'm actually being serious and want answers. "Your grandfather found out about the trouble that Martin was in and decided to help him out." She shakes her head. "Your grandfather went against your father's wishes and introduced him into family. There's only a handful of people who knew that Martin was your father's son, those people were sworn to secrecy. Your dad was livid but couldn't do anything as your grandfather was the boss and he had to do as he said but god he hated it."

"How did Martin find out about Dad being his dad?" I ask, and it's something that I've yet to work out.

Mom shrugs. "I'm sorry son, that's something that I don't know. You're going to have to ask your father."

I walk over and take a seat beside Mia. "Mom do you think dad can be trusted?" I'm asking her because after everything she's been through with him, with her being part of this life, his life, she will answer me truthfully.

"Trusted on what? That's a loaded question, Hudson." She releases Mia's hand, and sits back in her chair. "Can your dad be trusted in a relationship? God, no. Can he be trusted with a secret? Now, that's debatable…"

I decide to just ask her what I need to know. "Can he be trusted with my life? Will he betray me?"

She doesn't even hesitate. "Never, he would never betray you. You are his pride and joy, whoever put that thought in your head is wrong. There is one thing in this life your dad loves and I'm looking at it right now," she tells me honestly and I nod. "Hudson, your father is a lot of things but he would never betray you or the family."

"So he wouldn't help Martin?"

She frowns. "Over you? Never. He'd die first."

That's what I thought but so much has happened that I'm doubting everyone.

"Hudson, trust your gut," Mom tells me. "It's time to eat." She rises from her chair and walks into the kitchen.

"You okay, Princess?"

She nods, a massive smile on her face, she looks breath taking. "I like your mom. She's sweet."

I laugh. "Mom and sweet don't go together. Come on, let's go and eat before it goes cold." I get to my feet and pull Mia up, she crashes into my body and I take this opportunity to press my lips down against hers and kiss her.

EIGHTEEN

Mia

I DON'T HAVE LONG, I promised Jagger I would be quick. If Hudson knew that Jagger had left me alone he'd go crazy, but right now I cannot have Jagger in the store with me. I told him I need to grab some sanitary towels; as soon as the words left my mouth, I knew he wouldn't be coming with me. The way his face blanched and his body cringed, a typical male way of dealing with what goes on in a woman's body.

Rushing down the aisles, trying to find what I came in for. Quickly picking up some sanitary towels and throwing them in the basket. While I'm here I grab some shampoo and conditioner, basic things that I don't have at Hudson's. He bought me a different brand than I usually get and the soap he bought me has irritated my skin and I have a little rash. It's sore and I'm hoping using my usual brand will ease it. Since today is the first day I've been set free, not having Hudson around me all the time. It's what I said to Hudson this morning, he didn't find it amusing. Finally I come down the aisle I've been searching for. I don't even look I just pick up a box and throw into my basket. I quickly rush to the counter, knowing that Jagger could be walking in any second.

The cashier starts ringing through the order when she comes to the box I picked up. She gives me a curious look, I close my eyes and ignore it, not wanting to talk about it and not wanting to think about it. Thankfully the cashier doesn't say anything and I pay and dash out of the store.

Sliding into the car I place the bags out my feet. "Did you get what you needed?" Jagger asks softly, he's so sweet. He's got a glint in his eye now that Sarah's back, he's so happy.

"Thanks for bringing me, Jag."

He shrugs as he puts the car into drive, there goes my freedom, it's time to go home. "You're welcome, just don't say anything to Hudson, if he knew that I let you out by yourself he'd blow a gasket."

I laugh knowing damn well he would. "Cross my heart, your secret is safe with me. How are Allie and Sarah?" I always ask him this every time he comes to the house or when he's babysitting me. It's the first thing out of my mouth. I always ask how my girls are, I'm sad because I haven't been able to see them since Lacey's funeral, but I also understand why. Being around me could put them in danger and I would never want that so I agreed with the men, to keep them safe, we have to be apart.

"They're good although I know you know that. It's not like you two don't talk." He shakes his head at me.

It's true, Sarah and I FaceTime every day, maybe two or three times a day. I need my friend and she needs me, I still haven't told her what happened and I don't know if she knows. I haven't quite been able to approach the question with Jagger, but I know that I need to ask him. I don't want her to know, not just yet anyway

"Jag?" I question.

"Mia," he replies with a smirk.

"Did you tell Sarah what happened in that basement?" There it's out now.

He's silent for a second. "Mia what happened to you in that basement is your story to tell. I would never tell Sarah something that you need to tell her. I am going to keep it a secret until you are ready to open up to her." He reassures me but there's also a grit to his tone.

"You think I should tell her?" I asked quietly, I'm not sure if I'm ready for that.

He nods instantly. "Yes, I do think you should tell her but I don't think you should tell her until you're ready. I understand that has to be hard for you, I also think that by not telling her you're not allowing yourself to come to terms with what has happened. You're strong, there is no denying that. We're all in awe of your strength and resilience. But Mia sometimes you need to let it out and you haven't…"

"I have." I cut him off, "I have come to terms with it."

He shakes his head. "No Mia, you haven't come to terms with what he has done to you." He says softly, "He violated you, he took something from you. Maybe talking to Sarah may help you deal with that, I don't know but I do believe you should talk to someone."

"Okay," I reply, unsure what to do. I love that he's worried but I just don't know if I have it in me to talk about it.

"Have you spoken to Hudson about it?"

I frown. "I told him everything," I reply, although I didn't tell him absolutely everything. Well mostly everything that happened.

"That's good, but Mia, did you tell him how you feel about it?"

I turn and face out the window just as the tears stream

down my face. "I don't want to. I don't want to tell him that, for him to hear it."

"Why? You're his fiancé, soon to be wife, don't you think you should be honest."

"I love Hudson, he's so strong, and he always knows what to do. He would never let someone hurt him the way that Martin hurt me. I feel weak and I feel dirty but I could never tell him because I don't want him to look at me like I'm weak and dirty." The tears cascade down my face, I'm unable to see as they come thick and fast.

"My god Mia," he gasps sounding hurt, but I don't turn to look at him. "Hudson loves you and I don't mean love as a generic term. I mean that man adores you, he worships the ground you walk on and he's not going to think you're weak and dirty he's going to think you're brave and amazing."

Everything I fear just rushes out of me. "I have this sense of dread that if I tell him everything I feel, that he'll change how he sees me. I don't think he'll treat me as the woman I am, but as a fragile person. I won't be treated like I'm broken." I wipe the tears away, willing them to stop. "Can we please just stop talking about this?"

"Yeah, of course. But promise me you're thinking about talking to either Sarah or Hudson? I don't like keeping secrets from her, we've promised no more. She's going to be really hurt that we both kept it from her but I'm willing to take that hit because you deserve to tell her in your own time."

I nod, still unable to face him as the tears drench my face. "I understand and I respect you for not saying anything. Thank you, Jagger."

"Anything you need, just ask. I mean that Mia, you just need to ask and if it's in my power then I'll do it. Let's get you home."

"Yeah, I'm tired." It's not a lie, I'm having a hard time sleeping, and I'm constantly fatigued. Anytime that Hudson leaves the house while I'm in bed, I wake up instantly and go into the sitting room. I can't sleep alone. It's stupid, I'm like a child.

"Close your eyes and rest, Mia, we've got a couple of minutes before you're home. Sleep. You're safe here," he whispers as the music lowers.

I yawn. "Thank you," I reply and close my eyes, I'm not holding out any hope but I'll stay quiet.

"Hey sleepyhead." That deep voice pulls me from my sleep, blinking, I see that it's Hudson. Why is he here? Where am I?

"You were asleep, you're home now. Come on, let's get you inside," he tells me as he lifts me out of the car, I wrap my arms around him and bury my head in his chest. My eyes close and I drift back to sleep.

Deep voices sound and I snuggle deeper into Hudson, wanting to block out the sound.

Stretching, I yawn. God, how long was I asleep? I don't hear the voices anymore. Opening my eyes, the light from the en-suite shines into the room. Movement from beside me has me turning to see him.

"Hey you. Did you have a good sleep?" he asks, his laptop on the bed, he's been working while I've slept.

"I did, what time is it?" I sit up and yawn.

"Almost dinner time. Are you hungry?" His voice is soft, almost as if he doesn't want to talk too loud while I'm still in a state of sleepiness.

My stomach growls on cue and I laugh. "I'm so hungry I didn't really eat much today. I've slept for so long. Have you been beside me all the time?" I question, feeling bad that he has.

"Of course, where would I go?" He answers as if it's normal.

"Don't you have work to do? Or do you not need to go to the club? You haven't been there in a while." I'm keeping him from doing his work, this is why I wouldn't tell him what I'm feeling, he's already sacrificing enough for me.

"Mia, relax okay. I don't need to go to the club. It's what I have a manager for. He will call me if they need me, my main focus is on you at the moment. You can't sleep unless I'm with you or Jagger by the look of things." He has a bite to his tone, is he angry? "So until we can get you sleeping again I am going to stay with you. You need to sleep, you haven't slept very much lately."

I lean against him and he instantly puts his arm around me pulling me closer to him. "I trust Jagger, Hudson, that's why I was able to sleep. Nothing else." I'm upset that he's mad that I slept while I was in a car.

"I know, I'm just pissed that you spoke to him instead of me."

I frown. "What?"

"Mia, you told him things today."

I gasp. "He told you?" I pull away from him, wondering what exactly he told him.

"Yes, Mia, you're not dirty and you're not weak." His tone hard, I never wanted him to find out.

I climb out of bed, his arms reaching for me but I rush for the door, needing to breathe, and needing water. I come to a stop when I walk into the living room, Jagger and Harrison are sitting down talking.

"Mia…" Hudson calls after me and both Harrison and Jagger turn to face me.

"Mia, are you okay?" Jagger asks getting to his feet.

I shake my head, disgusted that he'd tell Hudson. "I told you those things in confidence. You betrayed me." I spit out, tears falling. "I never wanted Hudson to know that I was weak, that I'm pathetic but you couldn't wait to tell him could you?" I scream. "I hate you." I rush toward the front door, needing to get away. Unable to stand being in the house.

My bare feet hit the ground and I don't stop, I rush around the back of the house knowing that I can't leave, I'm angry not stupid. The tears keep falling, but I keep running, there's a swing in the back, Hudson bought it for me last week, it's somewhere I come to think. As soon as I sit, I sob. Everything I've felt in the past month comes flooding out.

Bringing my legs up, I let it all out.

"Mia." The softness of his voice is unlike anything I've ever heard from him before. "Fuck, Princess, please don't cry."

I don't turn to face him, it's bad enough that he knows things I didn't.

"Princess, talk to me," he pleads, lifting me from the swing and into his arms.

"I didn't want you to know." I sob.

"Why?" He sounds so hurt.

"I didn't want you to not love me anymore." It sounds pathetic now that I've said it out loud.

"That's impossible, you're mine Mia, and that's never going to change."

"I can't get clean, Hudson. I can't wash him off me."

A growling sound sends shivers down my spine. "You will, I swear to you, Baby, you will feel as though you're clean. You already are."

"I feel weak, that I allowed him to do it to me. That I

wasn't strong enough to fight him off." I rest my head against his shoulder and sob. "Hudson, every time I close my eyes and you're not with me, he's there. He's touching me, hurting me, violating me. It doesn't stop."

Wetness hits my shoulder and I know that I'm not the only one crying. "Oh fuck," he gasps, "Baby." He's unable to make full sentences.

He holds me tight in his arms and waits for me until my tears finally stop.

"Okay, Princess," he says once my tears finally dry up. "I'm going to say something and I want you to listen without interrupting."

I nod, unable to speak.

"Good, firstly, I have never nor will I ever consider you weak. You are fucking strong, you're amazing. Look at you, you have been through hell and you're still standing. You're a warrior."

My tears begin to fall again, this time they're happy tears.

"You're not dirty, and would never be. You've been hurt in a way no woman should ever be. That's going to take a while to heal from and I'm going to show you every day just how fucking amazing you are. There's not going to be a day that goes by where you doubt my love, my commitment, my admiration for you."

"God." I breathe, he needs to stop.

"No, Princess, Hudson." I smile at his words, "I'm going to worship you in the dark, replacing those memories you have of him." I lift my head to look at him, those brown eyes of his so bright. He presses a kiss against my lips. "You're beautiful Mia. You took my breath away the first night I saw you, I fell in love that night. My feelings for you have only grown stronger since then."

"I love you. Words can't describe just how much I do."

"Made for me," He growls against my lips. "Lets' go inside. You need to eat."

I tense as I get to my feet. "Mia, you're going to have to talk to him."

"No, I don't. Not yet. I wasn't ready to talk and by him telling you, he made me. He took my choice away from me." I know that I have to talk to him at some point, but not right now.

"Okay," he says and I know that he wants to say more, he just doesn't want to push me.

He holds my hand as we walk back into the house, my heart galloping as we do. I know that Jagger's still here, his trucks parked out front.

"Mia," he says as soon as Hudson and I go into the sitting room. I look at him, he looks gutted. "I'm sorry, but Hudson needed to know."

"Yes he did, but not by you. Never by you."

His eyes widen, "Mia…"

"No, Jagger, I trusted you, I spoke to you in confidence and you broke that."

He closes his eyes, a look of pain etched on his face. "I'm sorry, but he deserved to know, you need help, Mia."

"You betrayed me. I told you that I didn't want anyone to know, you went against what I wanted. You took my right to keep a secret. Why do men take things that don't belong to them?" I don't know who I'm talking to, I'm just musing out loud now.

"I'm sorry, Mia."

I shrug. "It's done now, there's nothing I can do about it. Have you told Sarah?"

"No, I told you I wouldn't."

I nod. "Okay." I turn to Hudson, "I'm going to go and have a shower."

He kisses my head. "I'll order us some dinner. I put the

bag you got at the store in the bathroom. I didn't put anything away, I'll let you do that." He laughs and I'm relieved, he didn't look inside the bag.

"Thank you." I place a kiss against his lips and leave the room, glad to be getting the reprieve.

I empty the bag from the store, hiding the box as I do so. Once I have that done, I switch on the shower, stripping out of my clothes.

I rinse the conditioner out of my hair and stand under the stream of water, loving the way the water pounds on my back. Hands slip around my waist and up my stomach toward my breasts. His lips on my neck, kissing, sucking, biting.

"Hudson," I moan. "What are you doing?" I gasp.

"Worshiping you," he tells me and I lean my head back against his chest, letting him do whatever he wants. His dick hard against my ass, as he kneads my breasts. "Every. Inch. Of. You." He promises me and I want it, everything he's promising, I want it all.

"Please," I beg.

"Princess, patience is a virtue," he whispers against my ear, sending shivers down my spine and goose bumps to break out across my skin. His lips graze the outer shell of my ear before his teeth bite my earlobe.

I reach behind me, wrapping my hand around his erect dick, it's thick in my hand and I squeeze, loving the hiss he releases. When I begin to move my hand, he groans, "Fuck." He spins me around, lifting me as he does. My legs wrap around his waist as my hands go to his hair. "Gorgeous," he growls as he pushes into me. "Every inch of you, gorgeous."

I whimper as he thrusts hard into me. "Hudson."

"You're perfect," he tells me as he thrusts harder. "Made for me."

My heart bursts with love, this man is beyond amazing and he's all mine.

"Perfect...Clean...Gorgeous...Amazing." Each word with each thrust. "Beautiful..." he growls and I know that he's getting close, as am I.

"Love you." I breathe, and he thrusts once more inside of me and I explode. "Hudson," I cry out, gripping him tightly. He thrusts once more and cums, my name a groan on his lips.

NINETEEN

Mia

———

WALKING OUT OF THE BEDROOM, the aroma of Chinese food wafts through to me. My stomach growls, today hasn't been a good day. I need to apologize to Hudson, Harrison, and Jagger. While Jagger shouldn't have said anything to Hudson, he did and there was nothing that I can do about it, I'm actually grateful he did. Hudson and I are closer, I've been honest with him about everything.

As I enter the sitting room, I see Jagger and Harrison are still here. Both have a beer in their hands. Heat begins to rise in my cheeks, did they hear us in the shower?

"You okay, Mia?" Harrison asks, a worried look on his face.

I nod. "Yes, I'm sorry for the way I acted earlier."

"Don't apologize, if anyone needs to it's this asshole here." He nods his head toward Jagger and elbows him.

Jagger stands, he tentatively takes a step toward me and I smile, letting him know that it's okay. His arms go around me and he pulls me toward him. "I fucked up," he whispers, "I'm sorry Mia, I should have kept my big mouth shut."

"Please don't apologize, its okay. I shouldn't have shouted at you. I acted like a child when I shouldn't have. I'm sorry, Jagger."

"How about forgetting about it?" Hudson's voice calls out and I take a step back from Jagger to see him standing there with two plates in his hands.

"Boy, where's my plate?" Harrison asks him.

I smile and take a seat on the empty sofa. "In the kitchen, old man. You know where it is, you've got legs that work, use them." Hudson replies, walking over to me and handing me a plate, followed by a knife and fork.

"I see how it is, I've been demoted." Harrison says tongue in cheek, since he and mom have been apart he's happier, I like him this way, he and Hudson get along better.

"You were never in the lead to be demoted. Go get your dinner." Hudson tells him as he sits down beside me. "You okay?" he asks when the men leave the room.

"Yeah, I just wanted to apologize to them, I overreacted and I shouldn't have shouted at him."

"Princess, you had every right to react how you did. Jagger knows that if I had found out about that conversation and he hadn't told me…"

"He would have kneecapped me." Jagger laughs walking back into the sitting room.

"Too fucking right I would have, you would have kept your life though." Hudson replies as if this conversation is normal.

Just as we all begin to eat the doorbell sounds my body tenses. Who's at the door, we aren't expecting anyone. Jagger places his plate down on the table and gets to his feet. "I'll get it."

Hudson and Harrison continue to eat but my eyes are glued to the door Jagger has just walked out of. Worry is eating away at me, what if it's Martin? What if he's here? Hudson squeezes my knee as if he's trying to reassure me that everything's going to be okay. I give him a weak smile one that he sees straight through he doesn't say anything. What can he say? Until Martin is gone I will be feeling like this every time the phone rings or the doorbell sounds.

The door closes and I sigh in relief, whoever it was, is gone. When Jagger walks back into the sitting room, my mouth opens in shock as I see who is with him...My mom.

"Well this is cozy, now isn't it?" Her tone is full of anger and sarcasm. Hudson grips my knee tighter, she always goes too far. She never thinks before she speaks and every time she does she just come across mad and bitchy.

"Is there a reason you're here, Tina?" Harrison asks her, his voice deep and deadly I've never heard him speak to my mom like that before.

"I would like to see my daughter without making an appointment," she replies dismissing him.

"There's a reason you have to make an appointment Tina," Hudson says through gritted teeth. "Martin is still out there, he's lying low at the moment, but we don't know when he's going to attack next or who." I know that Hudson feels guilt that Martin hurt me, and for him not to be captured yet. Everyone Martin hurts, Hudson feels that deeply.

"You're meant to be protecting my daughter, but ever since she met you all you have done is caused her pain and sadness," Mom says, and smiles as Hudson flinches.

"No, he hasn't. Since I met Hudson, I finally feel happy and loved," I tell her, my fingers interlacing with Hudson's.

"Love?" she scoffs, "there's no such thing as love. Men

use and abuse you." Her eyes glancing at Harrison as she says those words.

"Mom!" I yell. "How can you say those things? Harrison was nothing but sweet to you, he gave you everything you asked for, everything you wanted and you threw it in his face by not accepting his son. You never gave Hudson a chance, you never even tried getting to know him."

"Mia, it's fine," Harrison tells me. "Your mom's here for an argument and I'm not going to give her the satisfaction, I've had enough of her bullshit to last me a lifetime."

"Tina, it's time for you to leave," Hudson tells her and I'm actually proud of both him and Harrison, the way Mom's talking to them and yet they don't respond with anger, they've so far kept their cool.

"I'm here to see my daughter, not her boyfriend," Mom's voice full of disgust.

"Fiancé," Hudson growls, the sound rattling in his chest.

Mom knows that, I told her the very next day it happened, she never acknowledged me. Mom laughs, "Fiancé? It's never going to last. Not with a man like you and a girl like her."

"What's that supposed to mean?" Hudson spits out, he's barely holding onto his anger. Mom's pushing him too far now.

She rolls her eyes. "What I mean is, Mia is sweet and you're well…. A criminal. Look at you, you've been with fifty women? Probably double that. Whereas my daughter isn't one of the whores you're used to. What's going to happen when you get bored? What's going to happen to Mia once you do?"

"Tina, it's time for you to leave." There's an edge to Harrison's voice, he gets to his feet and towers over mom.

"No, I won't leave. I'm finally telling you how it is. Someone is finally standing up to you, you're not getting away with what you're doing to my daughter." Pointing her finger at Hudson, a scowl on her face.

"Mom!" I yell, unable to believe the words coming out of her mouth. I have never seen her so disrespectful, not just toward Hudson and Harrison but to me too. "Just leave, Mom." I tell her not wanting to be around her right now. I don't even recognize the woman standing in front of me.

She gets a furrow between her brows. "Mia you can't be serious?"

I place my plate down on the table and I clasp my hands on my lap as I look at her. "Yes, Mom, I am." I reply. "Mom, you're standing here, being so disrespectful toward everyone. I met Hudson two years ago and he took my breath away. He made me feel something I have never felt before my life. I not only left, I moved to another state, every day for those two years he was all I thought about. He was my biggest regret. Imagine my surprise walking into your wedding celebration and you introducing him to me as my new stepbrother. It was as though fate had brought us back together. What you don't seem to realize is that every day since your party he has made me feel loved. If I ever have a daughter, I would want someone to make her feel the way that Hudson makes me feel and the fact that you can't see that shows that you don't really give a shit about me. So please, Mom, I'm asking you nicely, please just go." My voice is shaky, but it had to be said, right now I'm focusing on me, on what makes me happy and that's Hudson.

She gasps. "Mia you're brainwashed."

Hudson's had enough. "Tina, you can either leave by

yourself or you can be escorted out. Either way your ass is getting out of my house now."

Harrison grips Mom's wrist, tugging on it as he leads her out of the house.

"Mia, fucking hell, I've never heard someone say something so beautiful", Jagger says, a stupid grin on his face.

"Shut up," I grumble, not really in the mood for praise.

"Princess, I love that you think that, but if we have a daughter, I can tell you that no man is ever getting with her," Hudson tells me putting his arm around me and pulling me into his body.

"No one will ever get the chance to get that close, just as they won't with Allie." Jagger smirks.

"You two can't be serious?"

"Deadly," they reply in unison. "Mia, your mom said it, we're criminals, we'll kill anyone who hurts our women and children."

I groan, god help Allie, she's screwed having Jagger for a dad and Hudson for an uncle, I can envision them killing any potential partners she may have. "I'm going to finish my dinner and then watch a movie. I want to forget about what just happened," I say, wanting all this shit to be over with.

"I'm up for a movie," Jagger tells us with a smile, "Lethal weapon?"

I frown, "Don't you want to go home to Sarah and Allie?"

He sighs. "I do, but they're not there tonight. They've gone to spend the night with Frankie, they're were at her mom's today."

"Oh God I can just imagine how that went."

He nods. "She said it was okay, her mom seems to have changed." He doesn't seem to buy it. "We'll see what happens, only time will tell."

"Lethal Weapon?" he asks hopefully and I nod with a smile.

"Like we had any other choice," Hudson tells him.

"You do have a choice, one, two, three, or four?" Jagger replies with a cheeky smile.

"Which one is Chris Rock in?" I ask, that's my favorite.

"Four," they respond together and I'm getting freaked out. "Four is my favorite too." Hudson tells me, passing me my plate.

I don't have the heart to tell him that I've lost my appetite. Jagger puts the movie on as the room descends in darkness, before the screen lights up. I place my plate back down on the table and bring my feet up onto the sofa and snuggle up against Hudson, it's not long before I close my eyes and sleep takes over.

---

*B*anging breaks through my sleep, causing me to wake with a start. My hand reaches out and connects with Hudson's bare chest. There's that banging noise again, my hand shakes Hudson's body and he groans, "Hudson." I call, shaking him once again.

"Princess, what's wrong?" He asks as his eyes pop open.

"Someone's banging on the door," I tell him and he immediately jumps out of bed, grabbing his pants and putting them on as he walks to the bedroom door. Swiping his t-shirt off the chair as he walks past it. "I'll be back in a minute," he tells me and I nod pulling the sheets up to my neck. I turn to the clock and see that it's seven in the morning. God, who is calling at this time in the morning?

Hudson returns to the bedroom a couple of minutes later, his expression blank, I can't read him but I do know that something has happened. "Hudson?" I ask, softly.

He walks over to the bed and sits down beside me. "I'm going to have to leave for a while. Someone's been shot and I need to go to the hospital to check on them. I won't be long."

I nod. "Who is it? Are they going to be okay?"

"We're not sure yet, it's touch and go right now. Aaron is going to stay with you while I'm gone. Dad and Jagger aren't here," he says and I nod, I've met Aaron a few times, he seems nice, he respects Hudson a lot, it shows on his face every time he speaks to him.

"Okay, I hope that everything's going to be okay," I tell him, hating that someone else is hurt in this stupid feud.

He kisses my head. "Me too, Princess, me too." He stands and quickly gets dressed, in his usual attire, black suit and a white shirt. "Get dressed, Baby, I don't want Aaron seeing your gorgeous body."

I roll my eyes. "I'm hardly going to walk out in my pajamas now am I?" I tell him sarcastically. "I'm going to have a shower and then I'll make some breakfast. Would he have some?"

Hudson nods. "That man eats more than Jagger. I'll call you when I'm on my way home." He places a soft and gentle kiss against my lips. "Love you princess, call me if you need me."

"Love you too, I'll see you later," I tell him as he leaves me in the bedroom.

Moments later, there's a knock on the door. "Hey Mia, I just wanted to let you know that I'm here and I'll be in the sitting room if you need anything." Aaron tells me through the door.

"Hey Aaron, I'm just going to have a shower, then I'll make us breakfast."

His stomach growls and I laugh, God, that was loud. "Sounds good. Yell if you need me."

"Will do," I tell him and get out of bed and walk into the en-suite bathroom, the room is already illuminated. My nerves kicking in now, I open the cupboard and immediately spot the bag I have hidden here. My stomach begins to flip, I can't even think about it right now, I just need to do it.

My hand shakily picks up the bag, pulling out the box, a tear slowly slides down my face. God, this can't be happening but I googled all the symptoms I had and every one is a symptom of pregnancy. The fatigue, the bloating, the nausea, the heartburn, the sensitive nipples, and crying for no reason. I don't want it to be true, but everything points to it, not to mention, I can't remember the last time I had a period.

Sitting on the toilet, I read the instructions, wanting to make sure I do it properly. I think I read them five times before I finally have the courage to take the test. Once I do, I leave the test on the sink and wait. I put a timer on my phone and set it for three minutes.

Those three minutes are the longest of my life all I do is stare at the time as it slowly goes down. Minute by minute my tears still fall, what if it's positive? What am I going to do? I really haven't let myself think about it before now, I was really wishing that what I have been feeling was due to stress, but when I realized I hadn't had a period in a while I knew I had to get a test to be on the safe side.

Beep, beep, beep, beep. My alarm goes off, and my heart leaps into my mouth. Placing my phone down I pick up the stick. Glancing at the little window, those two pink lines so clear to see. My mind can't quite comprehend what I'm seeing, reaching for the box, I read the instructions again. I scan the instructions, trying to see where it says what two pink lines mean. Throwing the box down, I quickly stand and turn around, lifting the lid to the toilet just in time to throw up.

I can't stop, I retch and dry heave, the enormity of what that test means.

I'm pregnant.

The tears fall as I sit on the floor and pull my knees to my chest and sob, I'm pregnant and I have no idea who the father is.

My baby could be the product of love, or the product of rape

Books by Brooke

The Kingpin Series:

Forbidden Lust

Dangerous Secrets

For those who have been waiting for this...

Forever Love is coming July 16th.

This is the final instalment in the Kingpin series and will bring Mia and Hudson's story to a close.

Pre-Order now

Mybook.to/Forever-Love

With their enemy still on the loose Hudson and Mia have the fight of their lives on their hands.

As the death toll rises, the need to protect their family becomes more urgent.

With danger lurking around every corner they find solace in each other until more secrets rock their world, and their future is now left in uncertainty.

Will Hudson rein as boss or will his enemy finally be his downfall?

All the ways you can follow Brooke

Website:
https://brookesummersautho.wixsite.com/website

Newsletter:
http://eepurl.com/gC1j8P

Join Brooke's Babes:
https://www.facebook.com/groups/BrookesBabes/

Acknowledgments

Jasmina: Without you, I'd be a mess! Thank you from the bottom of my heart!
Yashira: Thank you so much for all of your help and hard work, you're amazing and I'm so grateful to have you in my life.
Tiffany: I can't thank you enough for everything you've done to help me. You're a star!
Jen: Ah, you're fabulous! Thank you!
Krissy: As always, you've gone above and beyond for me! There are not enough words in this world to describe just how much you mean to me. Love you, muchly.
Wendy: Thank you, you're my sounding board, my friend, and always there to listen to me rant. I love you.

Sarah, Yashira, and Krissy: Thank you all so much for reading Dangerous Secrets and helping me make it into the book it is today.

And thank you to you, for reading this book.

Printed in Great Britain
by Amazon